With all my Heart, with all my Mind

With all my Heart, with all my Mind

Thirteen Stories About Growing Up Jewish

Edited by Sandy Asher

SIMON & SCHUSTER BOOKS FOR YOUNG READERS

SIMON & SCHUSTER BOOKS FOR YOUNG READERS
An imprint of Simon & Schuster Children's Publishing Division
1230 Avenue of the Americas, New York, New York 10020

With All My Heart, with All My Mind: Thirteen Stories About Growing up Jewish copyright © 1999 by
Sandy Asher

Book design by Lily Malcom
The text for this book is set in Goudy.
Printed and bound in the United States of America
10 9 8 7 6 5 4 3 2
Library of Congress Cataloging-in-Publication Data
With all my heart, with all my mind : thirteen stories about growing up Jewish / edited by Sandy Asher.
        p.   cm.
Summary: An anthology of original short stories about Jews coming of age by thirteen well-known
Jewish authors. Each story is followed by an interview with the author.
ISBN 0-689-82012-7
1. Children's stories, American. 2. Jews—Juvenile fiction. [1. Jews—Fiction. 2. Coming of age—Fiction.
3. Short stories.] I. Asher, Sandy.
[Fic]—dc21
98-47117
CIP
AC

For Rabbi Rita Sherwin,
Zachary Sherwin,
and the Temple Israel congregation,
"growing up Jewish"
together

Special thanks to the YIVO Institute for the use of its research facilities, to the book *What Is a Jew?*, by the late Rabbi Morris N. Kertzer, to my fellow Jewish authors for their stories and insights, and to this book's watchful shepherds: Wendy Schmalz, David Gale, John Rudolph, and Stephanie Owens Lurie.

וְאָהַבְתָּ אֵת ה׳ אֱלֹקֶיךָ בְּכָל־לְבָבְךָ וּבְכָל־נַפְשְׁךָ וּבְכָל־מְאֹדֶךָ.

"You shall love the Lord your God with all your heart,
with all your mind, and with all your might."

—Deuteronomy 6:5

CONTENTS

Introduction

by Sandy Asher

There was a time, or so I've been told, when life was simpler: Nice Jewish girls learned to keep kosher homes. A Jewish boy who reached the age of thirteen could announce with confidence at the conclusion of his Bar Mitzvah ceremony, "Today I am a man," and then step out into his community as a responsible and acknowledged adult.

Was it ever really that simple?

One thing's certain: It's not simple now. Almost everything has changed. The coming-of-age ceremony is as likely to be for a Bat Mitzvah as a Bar Mitzvah, the neighborhood surrounding the *shul*, synagogue, or temple is not necessarily Jewish, the family itself may not be entirely Jewish, and—if all that isn't enough to complicate matters—the question "What is a Jew?" is constantly up for debate.

Somehow, Jewish youngsters must pick their way through a murky maze of choices and find a strong, modern identity, answering the question "What is a Jew?" with a resounding "Today I am!"

This rather daunting task is reflected in the late comedian Sam Levinson's classic tale of a Bar Mitzvah boy so confused by the purpose of his day in the spotlight—"You'll get presents!" he's told. "You'll get presents!"—that, shaking at the *bimah*, he announces before God and the congregation, "Today I am a fountain pen."

Okay, so maybe it was never that simple. Humor at a solemn moment, deeper meaning in a burst of laughter, covenant and betrayal, accomplishment and persecution, devastation and survival—all make up the grand mosaic of Jewish existence. Within it, entire generations struggle to grow up strong in spite of, perhaps even because of, uncertainty.

And each of those generations is made up of individuals with insight, inspiration, answers, or questions to contribute to the effort. In this anthology, as in life, thirteen well-known Jewish authors continue to make their contributions, drawing new stories about growing up Jewish from their hearts, experiences, and imaginations. They are prizewinners all—honored with parents' and children's choice awards, the Edgar Award for mystery, the Sydney Taylor Award given by the Association of Jewish Libraries, the O. Henry Award, and the National Jewish Book Award, among many others. And they've created a delightful gallery of humorous, tragic, contemporary, historical, and even futuristic characters, each responding to the challenge of growing up Jewish in a uniquely personal way:

- At nearly thirteen, Andrew fits the traditional "Bar Mitzvah boy" mold, but in Jane Breskin Zalben's "'Take My Grandmother, Please,'" he has a Hebrew student of his own, Mr. Pearlstein, who happens to be old enough to be Andrew's grandfather. They're an "odd couple" with humor—and Andrew's grandmother—in common.

- In "David's Star" by Jacqueline Dembar Greene, Cara is a Sephardic Jewish teenager who works in an ice cream and sandwich shop and meekly passes for Italian—until her boss's anti-Semitism becomes too obvious to ignore.

- Gloria D. Miklowitz takes us behind the barricades of Masada to witness "The Last Days" of a courageous band of Jews under Roman siege, and to ponder their awful dilemma: Is it better to live as slaves or to die free?

- Merrill Joan Gerber's nonconformist Rachel searches for vintage clothing in her trademark color—black. Visiting what her more conservative mother dubs "The Dead Man's Store," Rachel finds the perfect shirt and a young biker with memorable blue eyes.

- In Eric A. Kimmel's story, Passover comes out of a barrel, and with it comes a new question: What's the connection between Passover and the word "Willow" imprinted on the family silverware? Yitzhak is determined to find out, but is there only one answer?

- One of six hundred talented colonists traveling by spaceship, Drew-David wonders what his contribution to the new settlement is meant to be. Author Sonia Levitin provides an intriguing possibility in "Fly Me to the Moon."

- "It's not the *stuff* that matters," Charlie's father tells him in Johanna Hurwitz's "Family History." "It's the tradition. The continuity of a line going back and back." On the brink of becoming a Bar Mitzvah, Charlie finds it's his turn to read an inspiring letter written by his great-grandfather.

- Ever wonder who invented dating? Or dancing? Was basketball once known as basketcoconut? In "Cain and Abel Double-Date" Susan Beth Pfeffer offers unlikely but hilarious moments not found in any other version of Genesis.

- On Rachel's Bat Mitzvah day, her beloved grandma Hannah's confusion and erratic behavior signal the beginning of a new relationship between them, one that moves the young narrator of Phyllis Shalant's "Pinch-Hitting" toward adulthood in unexpected ways.

- In "The Rag Doll," author Ruth Minsky Sender recreates the Lodz, Poland, of her childhood, recalling how the love of her family and encouragement of her teachers held at bay, if only for a while, anti-Semitism and the terrible darkness to come.

- It's not much of a present—a monogrammed diary—but Benjy Stein names it "Frank" and begins recording the hectic days leading up to his Bar Mitzvah. Eve B. Feldman's "Frank and Stein" reveals Benjy's hopes, fears, and very funny nightmares.

- "I will bless you if you release me," Jaci is told in her strangely haunting dream. How can she be wrestling with an angel, as her Orthodox classmate Isaac suggests, when she doesn't even believe in God? Carol Matas explores the mystery of faith in her story, "Wrestling with Angels."

- And in my own "The Heart of Buchanan," a small-town public school Christmas assembly forces Sarah to reconsider the importance of "fitting in." At what point does being accepted into a group mean losing touch with one's religious identity?

The interviews that follow these stories offer a rare and fascinating glimpse "behind the scenes," as the authors speak directly and frankly about their own lives, their writing, and the role "growing up Jewish" has played in each. Here you will see even more ways that individuals define and relate to their Jewishness. For some, being Jewish means ritual: The services chanted, holy days observed, and traditions honored resonate with Jewish life around the world and down through the ages. For others, meaning is found in social action, heeding the call to "repair the world." Still others respond most deeply to the injunction to "love the work of My hands," finding spirituality in the wonders of nature. And for many, a history of persecution, including the horrors of the Holocaust in our own century, intensifies the importance of linking past with present to ensure the future.

So—what is a Jew? It's not surprising that where constant study and interpretation are stressed, the search for an answer to that question has led to the saying, "Ask two Jews and you will get three opinions." Jews have been defined as members of a religion, a culture, a people, a civilization, and, in ancient times and modern Israel, a nation. Although most are Caucasian, Jews are not a race: There are Ethiopian Jews, Chinese Jews, and Mexican Indian Jews. There are Jewish citizens loyal to the governments of dozens of countries. The various branches of Judaism—Orthodox, Conservative, Reform, Reconstructionist—interpret the teachings of the Torah, the first five books of the Jewish Bible, in ways ranging from literal to liberal and recognize different religious leaders among themselves. There are atheists and agnostics who also consider themselves Jewish. From the Torah come systems of ethics and civil law as well as spiritual guidance.

The search for definition is part of the tradition. In the first century B.C.E., Rabbi Hillel was asked to define Judaism while standing on one foot. "What is hateful to thee, do not unto thy neighbor," he replied. "All the rest is commentary." And from the prophet Micah comes another attempt to distill the essence of Jewish life: "What doth the Lord require of thee? Only to act justly, to love mercy, and to walk humbly with thy God."

In spite of their differences, few Jews would argue with the idea that Judaism is a way of life, and that finding the best way to live Jewishly is a personal responsibility and has never been easy.

Tribulation and celebration, it's all brought to the table here, food for thought. You don't have to be a Bar or Bat Mitzvah to feast at this coming-of-age banquet. You don't even have to be Jewish. There's something for everyone. Read, discuss, debate, ponder. Judaism will continue to grow stronger because of it. And so will you.

Welcome. Enjoy. Shalom!

"Take My Grandmother, Please"

by Jane Breskin Zalben

It was a warm Saturday morning at the beginning of May—Mr. Pearlstein's Bar Mitzvah day. Lou Pearlstein was the upstairs neighbor in apartment 5B of our brownstone. Several years ago after my grandfather had died, Mr. Pearlstein started coming downstairs to the first floor where my grandma lived to have a glass of tea and *mandlebrot*. Sometimes, I'd hear his footsteps thumping past my front door, because my family lived in between them, and I'd make some lame excuse to join them both downstairs.

I don't know if it was Mr. Pearlstein, his jokes, or both, that made me want to be with him. Maybe it was his bright blue eyes? They'd get all watery when he laughed. Tears would come out of the corners, and he'd wipe them with the white handkerchief he always kept tucked in his shirt pocket. His eyes reminded me of my grandpa's as they looked in the photographs of him Grandma still kept on the top of her mahogany dresser.

This particular Saturday morning was kind of special because Mr. Pearlstein and I had struck up a deal after he and Grandma Rose started getting real friendly. Since he had never become a Bar Mitzvah, and I was in the midst of studying for mine, I would give him Hebrew lessons. In exchange, he'd fill me in on his routine from the old days.

He had been the warm-up act for Henny Youngman in vaudeville, and I wanted to be a comedian someday. I don't know if it was a match made in heaven, but our pact seemed to work.

There was a lot of motion in the air—just like when my mother and grandmother cooked together in our kitchen for the Jewish holidays. No one stood still for a minute. Grandma was such a nutcase about Mr. Pearlstein's big day that she ran upstairs a few times to our apartment asking, "Should I redo my bangs? I must have slept the wrong way. I look like a porcupine. How's my dress? Not too short? I want to look my age."

I wanted out of here, so I went upstairs to check on Mr. Pearlstein and see how *he* was doing while my mother took the blow-dryer to Grandma's bangs. I mean, it was *his* Bar Mitzvah.

He opened the door. "Hi, Andrew."

"You look taller today," I said, staring at him in his navy blue suit. This was the first time I had ever seen him all decked out.

"Maybe I grew, who knows?" he teased as he bent over and adjusted my tie a little, near the knot. "Now it's straight."

"Are you nervous?" I asked.

"With a teacher like I had, who could be nervous?"

I looked down and smiled. "Well, as they say in the business, break a leg."

"Thanks, *boychik.*" He shook my hand. "Before you go, I want to show you something. Come on in."

Some eggplant-colored tulips from Grandpa's prizewinning garden that he had planted in the backyard over the years were in a crystal vase in the center of a table. Mr. Pearlstein saw me eyeing them. "Your grandma, Rose, gave them to me."

Next to the tulips was a thick blue-velvet pouch with gold embroidery on the front. He unzipped it. "What's this?" I asked.

"Your grandmother also lent this to me last night. It was your grandfather's tallis. Could you believe I forgot to get one?"

"Grandma gave you his prayer shawl? I thought he was buried in it?"

"He was—with the one he wore in temple. This is the one he was called to the Torah in when he was bar mitzvahed. He also wore it when he married your grandmother. I hope you don't mind. It's only a loan." I shifted from side to side and shook my head no. "Because if you do, I won't wear it."

"No, I don't think I mind." I examined the black stripes and the white silk tassels at the ends. Then I felt the silver threads near where Grandpa's neck would have been. His skin had touched this very spot. I put my finger on a vine of twisted flowers and left it there.

Mr. Pearlstein put the tallis around my shoulders, and it drooped way past my knees. He laughed. "When you're thirteen, and it's your Bar Mitzvah, I know your grandmother will want to pass it on to you. I could also get you your own. There are these great little places in Brooklyn where the men who sew them make me look like a young-ster. I'll take you there. It's always nice having two." I liked the idea of Mr. Pearlstein still being in my life when I was thirteen. I hadn't thought about it. I hoped he would be. "So, is it a deal?"

I nodded. "It's a deal."

"So"—Mr. Pearlstein patted my back—"are you ready to go to *shul?*"

"I am," I said.

"Then so am I." Mr. Pearlstein and I walked downstairs together.

My parents and my little brother, Jason, were coming out of our apartment. "Do you know your lines?" Jason asked, looking up at Mr. Pearlstein.

My father began to shake his head and laugh. "I remember my Bar Mitzvah. It was in this old mansion off the boardwalk in Far Rock-away—a small hotel and catering hall with a synagogue in the base-ment. There was a sheet hanging up in the center to separate the men from the women. Orthodox Jews sit separately." He turned to Jason be-fore Jason asked his typical "Why?" "I said two words and the men in the congregation moaned, 'Oy, start over.' This happened about four, five times until my father's best friend yelled out, 'Give the kid a break.' *That* was my Bar Mitzvah."

Mom hugged Dad as she always did when he told this story.

"Well, with any luck, mine will go a little smoother." Mr. Pearlstein winked at me.

"I promise I won't make you do it over," Dad said, laughing.

"Good." Mr. Pearlstein began to laugh, too.

"Do what over?" Grandma Rose asked, coming out of her apartment and locking the door.

"You know," Mom said, "Hank's famous Bar Mitzvah story."

"Please"—Grandma threw her arms in the air—"don't put a *kineahora* on today."

"Evil eye," Mom muttered to us under her breath.

We all laughed. Mr. Pearlstein slipped a rose corsage on Grandma's wrist. Grandma looked down at the blue-velvet pouch Mr. Pearlstein was holding, and she touched it gently. "The best of everything," she said to him. "You deserve it."

Grandma Rose and Mr. Pearlstein walked to temple arm in arm. Jason and I were on either side of my mother and father. Grandma gave us each new yarmulkes before we went inside the synagogue. They were pale gray silk, and the name, Lou Pearlstein, and the date were embossed in silver on the cotton lining.

Gradually, the congregation filtered in. Mr. Pearlstein's crossword puzzle friends from the library came. So did his old vaudeville partner, Hymie Lindenbaum—all the way from Florida. Cantor Gold called Mr. Pearlstein up to the *bimah* and services began. I tried to imagine a young Mr. Pearlstein as an actor and comedian on the stage, but I couldn't.

There was an enormous wicker basket of flowers in front of the stand the Torah was on. The sun was shining through a stained-glass window above the ark. Tiny orange lights flickered on a side wall with the names of people on brass plaques, reminding us of those who had died. Grandpa's name was somewhere. And I let out a sigh. He would never see me standing up there on the *bimah* singing my haftorah. I think that would have given him a lot of joy. Then I looked at the opposite wall. A cloth woven with silver and gold threads was hanging, nearly covering half the wall. Grandma told me that it was called a *chuppa*, and she had helped sew it. During a wedding ceremony, the bride and groom stood under the *chuppa* canopy. "Someday, *alevai*." She poked me, motioning in its direction.

I rolled my eyes and said, "Oh, Grandma."

There was a lot of rising and sitting during the service. Grandma muttered to my mother as she put her hand to heart, "I haven't gotten this much exercise in a year. Who needs that aerobics class at the Y?"

At the end of the service, before the president of the congregation made the announcements for when candlelighting and services were next week, Rabbi Bloom called me up to the *bimah*. I was very surprised and broke into a hot sweat. My knees wobbled a little as I walked up to the pulpit where the rabbi and Mr. Pearlstein were waiting. I stood between them. Mr. Pearlstein gave me a nudge. The rabbi handed me a kiddush cup with my name engraved inside. "Andrew, you have been an excellent teacher, and a very patient one. Some of my Bar Mitzvah boys have not been as rambunctious as Mr. Pearlstein." Everyone in the congregation laughed. "It is of common practice in this synagogue to give the Bar Mitzvah boy his own kiddush cup, but Mr. Pearlstein insisted that we have it engraved for you. He told me, 'In this way, I'll always have to celebrate Shabbos with Andrew.'" Mr. Pearlstein patted my shoulder as I looked up at him. The rabbi continued, "May you have many *simchas* and may your parents have a lot of *nachas* over the years with blessings from this cup. Shabbat shalom." He shook my hand. And then Mr. Pearlstein's.

Mr. Pearlstein hugged me. "Good Shabbos," he said, beaming.

We went into a large ballroom next door, where a long table was set up with wine, challah, sponge and honey cake, and fruit for the kiddush. Rabbi Bloom said a prayer as the adults held up tiny cups of wine, and the children, grape juice, and then he cut the challah. Mr. Pearlstein cleared his throat and said, in his loud stage voice, a toast. "First, I want to thank you all for sharing this special day with me. I'd also like to say"—and as he stared straight at me my heart began to pound—"if it weren't for you, Andrew, we all wouldn't be here today celebrating. Thank you."

"*Mazel tov!*" everyone shouted.

As they were about to make a beeline for the food, Mr. Pearlstein added, "Not so fast. And second"—he held his glass high in the air, and looked at my grandmother—"Rose, darling, would you share the rest of my life? Marry me?"

Grandma looked as if she had choked on the hot horseradish she had on her piece of gefilte fish. She turned white and began to cough. "Lou, in front of the children?"

Trying to use what Mr. Pearlstein had taught me, I figured now's my time to do my stuff to save him from this awkward moment. "Boy, Mr. Pearlstein, the other day when I said, 'Take my grandmother, please,' I didn't know you were going to take me so seriously."

Everyone laughed. Then Mr. Pearlstein came over to me and placed both hands firmly on my shoulders. "Call me Lou."

"Call him Grandpa," Grandma said. "Only if you want to."

They both kissed me, one on one cheek, one on the other. I felt like a stuffed *derma* as they squooshed me between them. Mr. Pearlstein's eyes twinkled like blue sapphires. Like my grandfather's.

"Grandpa," I repeated, "take my grandmother, please."

And he did. Right to the center of the floor where the entire family and group of friends linked together, forming a circle around them as we danced the hora.

Interview ∽ JANE BRESKIN ZALBEN

Where did you get the idea for "Take My Grandmother, Please"?
The idea comes directly from the death of my father. After his funeral, when we sat shivah, my older son, Alexander, who was nine at the time, started telling Henny Youngman jokes from a book he had gotten from his other grandfather, who had passed away six months prior. During that same year, a neighbor invited us to her father-in-law's second Bar Mitzvah. He was eighty-three years old. There was something tender, endearing, and funny about this to me. I had never heard about a second Bar Mitzvah for an older person. The writer in me combined these two events and a story emerged about a young boy who wants to be a comedian when he grows up and an elderly man who was a comedian and had never been a Bar Mitzvah. They help each other attain what each of them needs: Andrew—jokes, Mr. Pearlstein—Hebrew lessons.

My husband went to an Orthodox yeshiva growing up, and that, too, has filtered into my writing. Andrew's father's Bar Mitzvah is actually his experience.

Is the household in the story similar to the one you grew up in?
I placed the setting in my brother's brownstone in Manhattan so that Andrew, his family, his grandma, and Lou Pearlstein could all live in the same building under one roof—the way my mother grew up.

My household growing up wasn't a religious one. My mother was born in Bialystok, Poland, and my father in the United States. I think it was very important for my mother to assimilate, even though she came from a family of very famous rabbis. Some of her aunts had died in the Holocaust and she was probably scared and at the same time embarrassed by being an immigrant (she spoke only Yiddish till age five). My father was more into hard work and relaxing with gardening or playing handball than singing tropes from the Torah on Saturday mornings. So I don't ever remember being in a synagogue with my parents until the day I was married.

But my best friend's father was a cantor in a Conservative synagogue. My memories of going to *shul* are with them. Of course, we did celebrate all the holidays and I'd stay home from school. The house smelled of delicious odors wafting in the air for each and every one. So religion to me became stories around the Seder table, jokes told during Rosh Hashanah, smelling apples in a sukkah, and the excitement of preparing for those special events.

I have always loved being Jewish. Judaism is part of who I am. I read Jewish books, magazines, and newspapers, see Jewish movies, go to Jewish art shows and plays. Probably the culture to me is the religious experience. Klezmer music gives me tingles. Yiddish words make me smile deep down to my bones. I also feel that this intensity is felt by many ethnic groups of many religions and what it boils down to is the warmth and closeness that families experience during holidays and during times of spiritual moments. Those moments are personal for each family. And within each family, each member determines what religion is to him or her. To me it can be a violin concerto, a flower with petals so blue or purple that you wonder how something so beautiful can exist on this earth, or just staring at the rhythm of ocean waves. It sounds corny, but often, that is a religious experience for me. And it would be unfair to limit it to just one religion.

In spite of Andrew's love for his grandfather, he's able to open his heart to Mr. Pearlstein without reservation. Can you talk about how that relates to growing up Jewish?
Part of the Jewish tradition of shivah is mourning, honoring the dead, and then moving on with life. Andrew doesn't forget his grandpa. He takes all the good feelings he has for him and finds another caring human being in Mr. Pearlstein so that he can relive joy, share an important life cycle, and learn things in a period of change. Through being loved, he can give love. Andrew is a mensch and performs a mitzvah in giving Mr. Pearlstein Hebrew lessons. If this isn't the tradition of Judaism, I don't know what is.

Biography ∽ JANE BRESKIN ZALBEN

Born in New York City, author-illustrator Jane Breskin Zalben began drawing seriously at the age of five and writing poetry for class newspapers in second grade. Three of her acclaimed picture books about Jewish holidays, inspired by her sons, Alexander and Jonathan, have been named *American Bookseller* "Pick of the Lists": *Beni's First Chanukah*, *Beni's Family Cookbook for the Jewish Holidays*, and *Happy New Year, Beni*. The series, which celebrated its tenth anniversary in 1998, has also earned Sydney Taylor Award Honor Book, and American Library Association Notable Children's Book, and CBC/IRA and Bank Street College of Education citations. Ms. Zalben's novels for older readers include *Water from the Moon* and *Unfinished Dreams*, which was nominated for the William Allen White Award. When she is not traveling around the country lecturing on children's books and encouraging young writers and artists, Ms. Zalben lives on Long Island, New York, with her husband and sons. Her son Alexander, who inspired this story, has been writing, directing, acting, and managing in a comedy troupe for four years. Mr. Pearlstein would say, "He should only earn a living; I wish him *mazel*."

David's Star

by Jacqueline Dembar Greene

I was carrying a tray of sundae dishes, hot out of the dishwasher, and nearly dropped it when I saw Sam. He wore a frilly white apron over his black chinos, and pink rubber gloves. Sam squatted in front of the empty stainless steel shelves where we stack clean dishes, wiping them with a cloth reeking of ammonia. His broad nose was wrinkled and his mouth pursed. Between the expression and the accessories, I burst out laughing.

Sam glared at me from behind his wire-rimmed glasses, his eyes watering from the ammonia fumes. "You think this is funny? Why don't you try it for a while?" I plunked the heavy tray onto the counter and drops of water puddled under it.

"You think our mighty manager never made me do that?" I asked. "Every time it gets slow in here, he finds some rotten chore for me. If my mother asked me to scrub our shelves with ammonia, I'd absolutely refuse. But here, I do whatever Dave commands."

"Maybe you do, Cara," he said, "but this isn't what I was hired for." Sam was a college student, premed, which certainly impressed me. He was even taking summer classes at a local university each morning, just to get ahead with his requirements.

He had only been working at Cameron's Ice Cream Shop for three weeks, but already he was complaining about everything. Of course, I agreed with him, and secretly admired his willingness to speak up to the manager. I griped privately to my friends, but never to Dave. At work, just as at school, I don't like to make waves.

Sam sloshed the smelly rag across the shelf, missing the back corners, and moved to the next. A gold six-pointed Jewish star dangled from his neck as he leaned over. That was another thing that marked a big difference between Sam and me. Sure, I'm Jewish, too, but I certainly wouldn't advertise it. Not at work, and especially, not at school. My grandmother had given me a necklace with a delicate silver Star of David, but it stays hidden under my clothes, except when I visit her. And with a name like Cara Matarasso, and my olive complexion, most people assume I'm Italian and Catholic.

Actually, our family is Spanish and Jewish, but I usually don't correct them. It's too hard to explain that we're Sephardic Jews, a branch of the religion most people have never heard of. Our customs are different, including prayer services in a combination of Spanish and Hebrew. And forget matzo ball soup. Our foods are Mediterranean dishes, like stuffed grape leaves, and rice cooked in tomato sauce. Not only am I different from my Christian friends, I feel different from other Jews. Believe me, it's a lot easier not to get into it at all.

I doubt there are half a dozen Jewish students at Wellburn High School, including me and my older sister. I'm careful not to invite friends over on Friday nights, just so I don't have to explain why my mother is lighting Sabbath candles. Then there's Passover, when we aren't allowed to eat anything with leavening for a whole week. Each spring my mother prepares for the holiday. She changes all the dishes, clears out any traces of bread or flour products, and goes into a cooking frenzy. That week, she sends me to school with matzo for lunch, along with a traditional spread she makes with dates and apricots. Not that it isn't delicious. But you can just picture it. Eating those flat boards of matzo would make me stand out as if I had walked into school with my hair dyed flaming orange. Instead, I leave them in my locker and buy a bowl of soup.

When Sam finished wiping, I started stacking sundae dishes, stem side up. Dave might not notice the spots Sam skipped with the cleaning rag, but he would definitely check the lineup of dishes.

Sam spoke more quietly now, as if what he had to say was only for my ears. "If everyone who worked here signed a petition asking for a few changes, we'd all be better off."

"Or out of work," I said. "Maybe you don't need this job, but I do." I could have explained my situation to him, but I kept my mouth shut. No point in advertising that my father had been laid off from the engine factory where he worked, and his benefits would run out soon. I offered my skimpy paycheck to my parents to help with household expenses, but Dad says he's keeping track of every penny I give him. He's going to put it all in my college account as soon as he gets a new job. And any tips I make are mine to keep. Not a bad deal.

Of course, when I started working at Cameron's, I had visions of getting large tips. I smiled at everyone, praised their kids, and stuck an extra cookie on the side of the sundae dish. But I learned one thing in my first day on the job besides how to make an ice cream soda. When you work at the counter, people don't tip much. They slide onto a stool, order a milk shake or a dish of ice cream, and rarely leave anything for the waitress.

And if you get stuck working at Take-Out, making ice cream cones and ringing up customers' checks, there is no jingle in your pocket at the end of the day. I had started there, and that's where Dave had stuck Sam for most of his three weeks on the job.

"I'm supposed to be a waiter," Sam had argued.

"No, you're supposed to be a worker," the manager snapped. "You'll work where I put you, or you can take a hike."

Tammy was the other waitress working today. She strolled from the back toward the shop's only four booths. Long Tall Tammy was a senior at Wellburn High, and because she had worked here the longest, or perhaps just because she knew how to sweet-talk Dave, the booths were her domain. That's where the real tips were. Tammy acted like she owned the place, and we were just her hired help. She slowly checked the sugar containers on each table. They were already full, because Dave had made me fill them. Then she poked at the napkin holders, which Dave already had me pack until they bulged.

It was now four in the afternoon. The frantic lunch hours were over, the afternoon ice cream crowd was gone, and the shop was empty. Yet Sam and I had been given extra work to do, while Tammy leaned against the counter and looked at her long red-polished nails. She smiled faintly in our direction and ran her fingers through her blond hair when Sam looked up.

"How can anyone look so good in that uniform?" he muttered.

"At least you get to wear black pants and a regular shirt," I said. "Well, most of the time, anyway. That apron really isn't you, Sam." It really wasn't me, either. I looked down at my sea green nylon uniform and the ruffled apron that went over it. At Tammy's statuesque height, at least the dress fit her. For me, at four feet eleven, the one-size-fits-all uniform didn't fit any of me, let alone all of me. We weren't allowed to make alterations, so I couldn't even shorten the hem.

"I could add uniforms to the petition, if you'd sign it," Sam offered. "I'd write: 'Waiters and waitresses will wear black pants and a white shirt.' Also, 'Workers will be given a food allowance to cover meals while on break.' I can't believe that Dastardly Dave makes us pay for our lunch. It's one more example of how he takes advantage of us!"

He was right about that one. And everything else Dave made us do. Like keeping the floors dry during busy times. Even though slippery floors were dangerous for us, Dave wouldn't hire enough people to have someone available to mop up when things spilled and dripped as we rushed around.

Then, of course, there was the issue of tips. Working the booths, Long Tall Tammy had large groups to wait on. They ordered meals and drinks and desserts. Then they left a fat tip.

"All tips should be shared," Sam had told me. I'd never heard of that before, but what do I know? This is my first real job. His idea was to have a jar into which all tips would be placed. At the end of each shift, the money would be divided equally. Since we are all helping one another, just working at different stations, it was only fair. Tammy had smiled indulgently at Sam when she heard that plan.

"I really don't think Dave would allow that," she purred. And when Sam approached him, the manager dismissed the idea completely. No doubt Tammy had gotten to him first and made sure she wouldn't lose any of her big tips. When she talked to the manager, he listened.

"I don't know about you," Sam said, "but I've just about had it with this place. On top of everything, Dastardly Dave keeps giving me morning shifts, when he knows I have classes. Then he yells at me for changing my hours." Even with the pink gloves and the apron, Sam looked kind of sophisticated and intelligent. Maybe it was his glasses.

I didn't say anything, but I really didn't want Sam to quit. I liked having him around, with what Dave called his "college boy ideas," and his bigger view of the world. I would never have the nerve to say anything to Dave about working conditions, or getting a crack at waitressing the booths, but having Sam around made me feel that maybe, sometime, I might.

A customer slid onto one of the stools at my counter. It had to be Mr. Spinelli, on his way home from work. He comes in every day around four fifteen and orders coffee, black. He plopped his work hat onto the stool next to him.

"Ah, Cara *mio*!" He grinned. "*Come stai?*"

"Honestly, Mr. Spinelli, I really don't speak Italian." I tell him that every day, but he still keeps speaking a few words of his native language to me.

"Nice Italian girl like you, Cara, you've got to learn."

I never argue with customers, especially about whether or not I'm Italian. It takes too much explaining, and I'm sure Mr. Spinelli wouldn't like it if I dumped the whole Sephardic thing on him.

"The usual?" I asked.

"Sure, sure." He nodded. "I need that cuppa coffee to keep me awake. After stacking stone walls all day, I can barely make it through dinner. The wife wouldn't like it if I fell asleep in the minestrone!"

I brought him coffee, and set out a napkin and a glass of water. Then I heard Dave tapping on the one-way glass that looked out over the restaurant. He can see us, but we can't see him. It's a creepy feeling knowing he can be watching you at any time. But when he wants us, he taps on the glass and we hear his presence, without seeing it. Like I said, kind of creepy.

I headed into the back room. Dave's office is across from the dishwasher and sinks, and from his one-way window, I could see Mr. Spinelli sipping his coffee and looking down at the counter with a tired gaze. A dirty gray carpet covered the office floor and there was a small photo tacked to the wall showing a grinning Dave holding up a glassy-eyed fish. It was probably his biggest triumph.

A large chalkboard outside Dave's door listed the shifts for each day of the week, so the workers knew their assignments. Today was Friday, and he was setting up the schedule for the coming week. Sam stomped past us and dumped the dirty ammonia in a work sink back near the ice cream freezers. I saw his name on the board for Take-Out, and during the morning shift. This was going to be trouble, but I kept quiet.

"Well, Cara, how would you like to work the booths this weekend?" Dave asked, as if he was sure it was a gift I couldn't refuse. But this was Memorial Day weekend, and my family planned to spend it at my grandmother's house near the ocean. I wasn't supposed to work at all. I was going to stretch out in the sun, as if I weren't dark enough. My friends admired how easily I tanned, and the fact I never got sunburned. Summer was the only time people complimented my complexion. My first impulse was to say I couldn't work, but then I thought about Dave's temper, and the tips I'd earn on a busy holiday weekend.

"Would I be working the booths all three days?" I asked. Sam headed to the men's room, probably to wash away as much of the ammonia smell as he could. I heard the door slam. "I was planning to go away with my family, but I'll work if I get the booths all weekend."

"That's the plan, Cara. I know you can handle it. And Tammy won't be in." So that was it. I only got the booths because Long Tall

Tammy wanted the weekend off. As if she needed a tan to be noticed. Well, so what? Maybe if I did a really good job, Dave would give me the assignment more often. I saw Mr. Spinelli put his cup down and look around. He needed either a refill or a check. Tammy was ignoring him.

"I've got to get back out to my customer," I said. "Put me down for the weekend, Dave." I grabbed the coffeepot and headed toward Mr. Spinelli, but he waved me away.

"*Ciao!*" he called. He dropped a handful of coins on the counter and headed toward the door. I saw that he had left enough to pay for the coffee, plus the same amount as a tip. My Italian prince.

"Wait, Mr. Spinelli! Your hat!" As he retrieved his scruffy canvas hat, he smiled again.

"Ah, Cara *mio*, if only I were ten years younger. . . ." He patted his hand against his chest, as if his heart were beating through his shirt.

We both laughed. If Mr. Spinelli were ten years younger, he'd probably be about my dad's age. I scooped up the coins and dumped the empty coffee cup and glass into a plastic bin under the counter. Sam would probably get stuck washing the dirty dishes, too. Dave really did seem to have it in for him, though I couldn't figure out why.

As I was ringing up Mr. Spinelli's check, I heard an argument in the back. Sam must have seen the new schedule. Tammy leaned herself gracefully against a booth and pretended not to notice. Sam stormed in and took up a place behind the Take-Out counter. A group of boys from the baseball team piled through the door, sweaty and rowdy. Their dank T-shirts read: WELLBURN BASEBALL—ALWAYS A HIT! They crowded around the counter, calling out ice cream flavors. Sam was going to be busy.

"I'll get some of those cones," I offered, but Sam barely acknowledged me.

"I've got it all under control," he said, dipping the metal scoop into the first bin of ice cream. His voice sounded angry and satisfied at the same time.

I looked at the clock. Only another half hour and my shift would

be done. My feet were prickly and tired, and I felt like my nylon uniform had absorbed the smell of every frying burger that had sizzled on
the grill. I was dreaming about a cool shower when I saw Sam stacking
huge piles of ice cream on each of the cones he was handing to the
baseball players. They were a lot bigger than we were supposed to
make. Then I heard staccato tapping on the one-way glass. I tried to
save Sam by going back myself.

"Not you, Cara!" Dave fumed. He pointed toward his window.
"Look at the size of those cones!" He rapped the glass harder, but Sam
didn't turn around, or stop heaping giant scoops of pistachio, chocolate, and fudge ripple ice cream.

The manager flopped into his chair and swiveled toward me. "I
knew he wouldn't make it," he said, spitting out his words. "You'll see,
he's gonna quit any day now." I was afraid to get involved with bad
feelings between Dave and Sam, but I really wanted Sam to stay.

"Well, maybe if you give him a better assignment," I suggested. My
heart was beating hard, and my palms felt sweaty. Why was I getting
involved in this mess? But I couldn't seem to stop myself. "And remember he needs to work afternoon shifts."

"Sweet little Cara," Dave smirked. He shook his head as if he
couldn't believe how naive I was. "It has nothing to do with any of
that." He leaned forward in his chair, as if he were about to educate
me. "It's because he's a Jew."

A cold spot grew in the pit of my stomach and began to spread. I
tried to say something, but no words came out.

"They're all like that," Dave went on, leaning back in his chair and
waving his hand toward the window. "Think they're too good for this
job. Big college boy," he sneered. And I just stood there, saying nothing, when I knew I should stop him. "They don't want to get their
hands dirty. Jews are all the same. They want the money, but without
doing the work."

I started to back out of the office, when the schedule board caught
my eye. White chalk letters gleamed in the flickering fluorescent light
and I saw my name written in for the weekend shift at the booths. It

was clear Dave didn't know I was Jewish, but how could he? I never dropped a clue. If I had told him, he wouldn't have said any of this to me. But would he still feel the same?

I remembered Mr. Spinelli thinking I was Italian, and how I'd never said I wasn't. I thought about Sam's Star of David dangling from his neck and mine hidden under my collar. Being Jewish wasn't something Sam talked about, it was just part of him. Like his willingness to stick his neck out so we all might have better working conditions. My face and neck felt hot, but the coldness in my stomach spread like fingers of ice cracking at the edge of a frozen pond.

"Don't I work hard and do the dirty jobs, too?" I asked, my voice sounding thin and whispery.

"You?" Dave's thick eyebrows knotted together. "I don't mean you, Cara. I'm talking about Jews." He spat out the word and it sounded ugly.

My voice rose slightly. "I work hard to earn my pay and my tips, too. I don't expect to get paid for nothing, do I?"

Dave scowled. "What are you talking about, Cara? I said I don't mean you. You are a terrific, dependable worker. That's why I'm putting you on the booths. In fact, you're a star employee." I tried to look Dave in the eye.

"And I'm Jewish," I said. His eyebrows lifted in surprise. Before he had a chance to make lame excuses, I walked out. The last baseball player trooped out, his ice cream heaped into a round crest, and the sides fanning out over the edge of the sugar cone. Sam was laughing, but with what had just happened, I couldn't join in. Then Dave came out, his face red with anger. Without me to distract him, he was ready to discipline Sam.

"You're fired!" he shouted.

"Oh, did I forget to tell you? I decided to quit half an hour ago," Sam said. He was still laughing. "That's why I couldn't charge anything for those cones. I didn't think a former employee should open the cash register." He hugged me, and I caught a faint, spicy whiff of cologne. "So long, Cara. Stick up for yourself." And that was it. Sam was gone.

As soon as my shift was over I stuffed the dirty apron into my pocket with my measly tips. As I walked past Dave's office, cloudy smudges of chalk dust blurred the schedule board. My name had been erased from Booths, and written instead under Take-Out. Another waitress's name appeared in my place. Dave was going to have me replace Sam this weekend, not Tammy.

Stick up for yourself, Sam had said. With my fingers, I smudged out my name, and the new one, and wrote *Cara* again under Booths. The chalk scraping across the board got Dave's attention. He cracked open his door.

"What do you think you're doing?" he bellowed. His face was hidden behind the half-opened door.

This time I wasn't afraid. I pushed open the door, but Dave wouldn't meet my eyes. Maybe he wanted me to quit, too, but I wouldn't give him the satisfaction. I remembered my grandmother saying Jews don't give up, or there wouldn't be any. I tugged my Star of David out from beneath my collar and let it dangle openly. After all, I was a star employee.

"See you tomorrow, Dave," I said, and walked out into the fresh air.

Interview ⌒ JACQUELINE DEMBAR GREENE

How close do the events in "David's Star" come to your own experiences growing up Jewish?

The first job I had was working in a local ice cream and sandwich shop just up the street from my house. I was sixteen years old. I remembered an incident there that had shocked and frightened me. A young Jewish college student had started work for the summer and was soon having constant arguments with the manager. I could see he wasn't being treated fairly. I couldn't understand why, until one moment when the manager told me that the young man wouldn't last long "because he was a Jew." As shaken as I was, I spoke to him in much the same words that Cara uses in the story. After announcing that I, too, was Jewish, I walked out.

In writing "David's Star," I dramatized the original incident. Some things about Cara, such as her physical characteristics, are based on truth. I really was still four feet eleven inches at age sixteen! All the characters in the story are fictionalized.

Cara mentions feeling different, even from other Jews. Did you feel that way, too?

Being one of the few Jewish residents in a small rural town, I always felt different from my neighbors and friends. Although I was proud of my religion, I was reluctant to share it with others. I was certain they wouldn't understand, and I felt it would only isolate me. In addition, my family was of Spanish-Jewish heritage, a branch of the religion called Sephardic. Even as I grew up and made more Jewish friends, I felt different from them. During the High Holy Days, while my friends attended large synagogues together, our family held a separate service with a small group of other Sephardic Jews. It was conducted in the combination of ancient Spanish and Hebrew called Ladino. Our family's foods were of Mediterranean style: rice with tomato sauce, homemade yogurt, lemony stuffed grape leaves, thick lentil soup.

Did your family come from Spain?
My grandparents were both born in a town that was part of Greece, and then Turkey, but they spoke Spanish, as did my mother and her large extended family. How could I explain that to anyone? I was too young to understand the long history that had led the Jews of Spain to countries like Turkey after they were banished from their homes during the Inquisition in 1492. Hundreds of years later, my family still identified with that heritage. They were still Spanish Jews.

How did your experience in that ice cream and sandwich shop affect your feelings about your heritage?
In many ways, this story reflects the long path of growing up, and learning to understand and appreciate who I was, and who I am. When I confronted the manager's prejudice, my understanding of my heritage became clearer. I knew where my loyalties were. I saw my place in the world with a different eye.

As an adult, I spent many hours learning more about Spanish Jews and their lives before and after the Inquisition that uprooted them. Because Sephardic Jews are small in number, particularly in the United States, it is a minority that needs more exposure and must work hard to preserve its books, distinct prayer services, and unique traditions. I enjoy using references to Sephardic Jews and their history in some of my works so that readers will be exposed to this heritage. I also hope that there are readers of Sephardic descent who will gain new understanding and pride in their own rich background. I hope readers can see that the first step in being accepted for who you are is to take pride in yourself. This doesn't just hold true for religion, but also for clothing, ethnic customs, language, and background.

Biography ⌒ JACQUELINE DEMBAR GREENE

Jacqueline Dembar Greene was raised in the rural town of Bloomfield, Connecticut. She received a B.A. in French literature from the University of Connecticut and an M.A. in English literature from Central Missouri State University. She has taught high school French and worked as a journalist for several Boston area newspapers. All of her books reflect a journalist's passion for research and attention to factual detail. Her picture book, *Butchers and Bakers, Rabbis and Kings*, was a finalist for the National Jewish Book Award. Among her historical novels for young adults, *The Leveller* was a *Booklist* "Pick of the Lists," and *Out of Many Waters* was named a Sydney Taylor Award Honor Book and a New York Public Library "Book for the Teen Age." Its companion novel, *One Foot Ashore*, was also a Sydney Taylor Honor Book and an *American Bookseller* "Pick of the Lists." Two of Ms. Greene's nonfiction books, *The Tohono O'odham* and *Powwow: A Good Day to Dance*, are illustrated with her own photographs. Ms. Greene is married, the mother of two grown sons, and lives in Wellesley, Massachusetts.

The Last Days

by Gloria D. Miklowitz

In the year A.D. 72 at the end of a brutal war lost to Rome, 960 Jewish men, women, and children fled Jerusalem in what was then Judea and escaped to Masada. A mountain fortress near the Dead Sea, Masada's only access was by a steep, narrow path that snaked up the mountainside to a high stone wall. Within those walls the Jews lived free and safe with plenty of food and water, but they continued to resist the Romans by attacking them wherever possible. The Roman emperor Vespasian ordered that Masada be taken, that those who resisted be killed, and that the rest be brought back to Rome as slaves. This is the story of Masada's last hours and the decision faced by a boy not quite thirteen.

I, Daniel, son of Eleazar, run from the storeroom of our fortress carrying arrows to our men on the ramparts. There is chaos now. My people race about like rats from a fire. Arrows rain skyward. A man's bloody head flies by, struck off by a stone the size and shape of a pomegranate. Dread feeds in my stomach like a hungry worm.

And then the boom of the battering ram begins again.

I want to clap my hands over my ears to block out the awful pounding. Though soon to be thirteen, I want to curl up like a babe in its mother's womb and hide from the terror.

Yesterday the Romans finished building the ramp up the mountain that leads to the walls that encircle and protect us. Today, whipped onward by their captors, our own people—slaves now—were forced to haul an iron tower up that ramp. And now Roman archers fire down on us from its high platform and we can do little harm in return. Worse, while arrows fly, the huge black battering ram swings from that tower against our wall, slamming against the stone with a constant, regular, terrible thud.

I dare not think what will happen when the ram breaks through. The Romans destroyed Jerusalem, and our Temple. I know firsthand of their brutality. Will I be able to kill when I am face-to-face with the enemy? If I am captured, would I want to live a slave for the rest of my days?

"Daniel!" my father, our leader, cries when I reach him. "The wall is giving!" I can see his mind racing as he turns to me. There is desperation and determination in that look and then a sudden wild thought. "Quick! Gather everyone. We must build another wall, of wood! Quick!"

I run to do his bidding, but I wonder what good will another wall do? If the ram can tear through stone, it would surely destroy wood! There is a swelling in my heart, like a well of tears. We are God's chosen people, yet God has forsaken us!

In the hours before darkness, before the stone outer wall is breached, all who can help do so. Fathers and sons, even the men who opposed my father earlier, even the rabbis, swarm over the ground, desperate to shore up our defenses. With hammers and axes we rip out the heavy beams that support the roofs of the palaces King Herod built on our fortress a hundred years before we came. We pull and carry and roll these huge beams across the plateau, ignoring the cries of the wounded, to where the Romans would break through. There, the beams are lifted and set in place to form twin walls, one behind the other.

At first I do not understand my father's intent, but there is no time to question. While the ram pounds at the outer stone, our men hurriedly raise these walls and I join others to fill buckets with sand. We hand the buckets to men on ladders who empty the sand in the space between. Now I see. When the battering ram hits the first wood wall, its pounding will shake the sand into a solid barrier between us and them!

I almost laugh with relief and joy at the ingenious plan. We buy time.

But how much?

There is a new sound now, the thud of the ram against wood, and with each thud our wall shivers but does not give. Again and again. And then suddenly, the pounding stops.

A cry of triumph fills the air as friend turns to friend to embrace. "Now they will give up," my cousin Aram cries.

"Do you think so, Daniel?" Deborah asks, almond-shaped eyes turning to me, begging for hope. I want to hold and comfort her, but we are not yet betrothed so it would be improper. I swallow the lump in my throat and nod, but look away. For months these Romans have lived on the desert floor thirteen hundred feet below us. They suffered from sandstorms and blazing heat and from lack of water. Still, day by day they built their camp, a wall around the base of our mountain to keep us from escape, and a ramp to our mountaintop. I shudder, knowing they will not give up, and hate myself for the fear and self-pity I feel. Will this be my last day of freedom? Of life?

It is not long after the pounding stops that we hear the swish of arrows slicing the air. This time the archers do not aim at us, but at the wood wall blocking them. Flaming arrows strike the wood and soon it is afire.

"The sand will put the fire out," Aram says.

"Daniel?" Deborah asks. "Will the sand do that?"

I take her hand. "Perhaps."

We stand watching, helpless. The fire burns hard and a wind sends the flames toward us so that it seems sure the inner wood will catch. The air is thick with burning embers and black smoke and the heat is great. I cannot keep my eyes from the fire as I edge through the crowd with Deborah, fingering the sword that hangs at my side. When the walls burn through, when the fire subsides, they will come, thousands against our few. How can I protect my little sister, Sara, or my mother? I have never killed. Can I stand face-to-face with the enemy and use my sword?

Near the storerooms a crowd has gathered around Rabbi Gamliel. I do not believe prayer will help. Think how we prayed to save our Temple in Jerusalem, yet the Romans took it. The rabbis say the Lord forsook us because we deliberately taunted our enemy by attacking their occupied towns. My father says it's a greater sin to remain safe in our haven and free while the Romans enslave our brothers.

"Oh, Daniel, look!" Deborah whispers, her voice rising in excitement. "The fire . . ."

I look where she points and see that the wind has shifted. My heart leaps. The wind now blows the flames away, back at the Romans, back at the iron tower! Back at the archers who set it ablaze. Has God heard our prayers, after all?

I make my way to my father and the men whose advice he relies on. As others cheer and shout, cry and laugh, praise our Lord for hearing their pleas, he stares at the flames without expression.

"Father?" I ask softly. "Do you think?"

"The wind will shift again," he says. "You can be sure."

"How long, Eleazar?" a man asks.

"Soon. But it is growing dark. They will wait until morning, until the flames subside. They can afford to wait, knowing we will still be here. Come, Daniel. Aram, you, too." He starts toward the small building that serves as headquarters. "Come. We have decisions to make."

And my father is right. Within the hour the wind shifts again and despite the sand, the thick inner wall is ablaze.

Sound carries far in this place. We hear laughter and celebrating from the soldiers below. General Flavius Silva, who has urged us to surrender many times, now taunts us. "Tomorrow," he calls to us, "you Jews will know the cost of thwarting the mighty power of Rome!"

My mother weeps as Silva's words fade; Sara clings to her, whimpering. The baby, Yoram, wails, sensing our fear. I force back tears, and speak encouraging words to them while all around us families gather, seeking comfort from one another. To whom can I turn? The end is near. I would be with Deborah, but she has gone to help with her wounded brother. And what could we say to each other, anyway?

"Enough!" my father calls out, commanding our people to still their wailing. He stands on the steps leading to the ramparts. While the fire crackles above us people hurry forth to hear his words, hoping for some scrap of hope.

"My friends . . . ," Eleazar, my father, begins. His hand trembles as he lifts it to his tired face. His voice is thick and low yet it reaches all. His eyes burn with a kind of certainty. "Friends," he begins again, "till this time we have run every risk to protect our freedom. We are the last to resist the enemy, but now we must expect terrible punishments if they take us alive. Vengeance will pour down on us. There is no doubt what tomorrow will bring. They will rape our women, send our children into slavery, and slay all who resist. Is this what we have fought for?

"It would be a favor if we can choose the death we would die, a favor refused to many of our people. Let us make our own terms and die free."

At these words there is a gasp of shock from those around me. My father holds up a hand for quiet, but it is some time before he can continue. "Yes, let us die free. But first let us set fire to the fortress and to our possessions—all but our store of food. Thus they will know we were not driven to this violent act by famine but chose death to slavery."

Oh, God. Oh, God! No! I think, my chest heaving with unshed tears. *How can he ask that? How can we kill our loved ones, ourselves? Jewish law forbids it! The rabbis will not permit it! I don't want to die. I have not lived! Oh, God. No!*

Around me families hug one another, sobbing. Angry voices ring out, but my father shakes his head. "All men die," he says, "both the coward and the brave. Do you think the Romans will forget that we had the courage to defy them—those who called themselves our masters?" He hesitates, waiting for his words to sink in.

"Imagine what it will be like for our old and our youth if we live to be enslaved. The old will die from their torments and the young will live only as long as their strength remains. Husbands must expect to watch the dishonor of their wives, and parents to behold their children begging for relief from their chains. These are things only cowards would permit—if they have the chance to forestall them by death!

"While freedom is ours and we are in possession of our swords, let us die free men, surrounded by our wives and children. And let us be quick about it so we snatch the prize from the hands of our enemies and leave them nothing to triumph over but the bodies of those who dared be their own executioners."

It is a terrible thing he asks. Life, no matter what kind, is better than death, isn't it?

Yet what he says of our fate is true. If we become their slaves, we will be forced to fight in the arenas for the entertainment of their people, forced to kill our own dear friends or fathers or be killed. Forced to work dark hours in salt mines for the rest of our days.

But knowing does little to ease the fear and revulsion at what must be done.

There is a frenzy of activity now. Men and women set fire to their worldly goods so that smoke and flames pour from their living quarters inside the stone walls. A huge bonfire burns in the middle of the plateau fed by clothing, linens, children's toys, precious possessions.

Suddenly I think—*Deborah! I must say good-bye!*

I leave my family and race across the plateau, unsure if I can find her in this mad scene. But she is in her family's abode, helping lift bedding from the ground to feed the fire.

"Deborah," I say. And without a word she leaves the room to join me outside. Her hair is wild; her face streaked with dirt; her eyes dark with fear.

"I thought . . . I feared you would not come, I would not see you before . . ."

Tradition, propriety no longer matter. I take her arms and bring her close, her slender body fitting against mine the way I dreamed of many times. "I had to come. I need to tell you what I feel. . . ."

She lays her fingers on my lips. "I know. I, too . . ."

My voice falters at her words. "Do not be afraid. It will be quick," I say. Tears run down my cheeks. "Perhaps, if there is a hereafter, we will be together again. . . ." I kiss her quickly and turn away.

Now comes the terrible time. Fathers embrace their wives and children, murmuring words of love, sobbing as they stab them and lay them side by side on the ground of their rooms. My father holds Sara close, then mother, and baby Yoram. I embrace each in turn, also, and bow my head, waiting for the blow that will end my life. But my father pushes me aside and does the deed to the others.

"Father?" I ask. "Why do you spare me?"

"Help me lay them to rest, and then I will explain, Daniel."

It is hard not to cry, not to scream, carrying my dead sister and brother to my mother's side. They appear to be sleeping though bloody from where their throats were cut. My father covers them with a bright cloth and says a brief prayer. His face is gaunt and the skin gray. His hand trembles as he wipes his sword and returns it to its sheath.

"Now," my father says, taking me aside and holding me by my arms. "This is what you must do."

I figure he will ask me to help others die who could not bring themselves to do the act and my skin crawls at the thought. But no. He asks of me something much worse.

"Someone must survive to tell the Romans why we have done this thing," he says. "To tell them that we die as free men, not as slaves. I ask you to be that one."

For an instant I feel jubilant that I might live, but then I cry, "No, Father. No! Do not ask me to abandon all those I love. I want to be with you and Mother. No! Do not ask this of me!" A picture takes form in my head of myself shackled in a cage drawn through the streets of Rome while people laugh and throw rocks at me. It is too awful to imagine.

"You must do this, Daniel. I know how hard it will be, but you are the one I choose. If no one survives to tell the world of our sacrifice, it will be for nothing. Someone must live to tell."

"Someone, but not me!" I beg. "I am only a child!"

"A child," he says, shaking his head sorrowfully. "Tomorrow, when the Romans arrive to attack, you will be thirteen with the responsibilities of a man. What I ask you to do takes great courage, Daniel. You must do it. Would they believe anyone but the son of Eleazar?"

And so it is that I must wait in the large cistern where the water is stored. My heart is sick from what I have seen and heard this night, and at what I must face tomorrow and the days to come. With me are two women and four children, hiding to avoid the fate of the others. Through the rest of the night we crouch. There is no sound from above, not a voice, not a footstep, not a cry of pain. The only sound we hear is the soft lapping of the water against stone. The only smells are those of smoke, mildew, and our own fear.

With morning, light seeps through the narrow opening from above. Soon I hear voices raised, shouts, heavy feet tramping overhead. A voice calls, "Hallo? Hallo? Anyone here?" My hands are icy and moist with fear. I rise from my crouching position and stretch my cramped muscles. "Come," I say, nodding to the others, and I start up the stairs.

Interview ⌒ GLORIA D. MIKLOWITZ

You've written a book about Masada, and now this story. What sparked your interest?

In 1965 I lived for three months in Israel, where my husband was a visiting scientist at the Weizmann Institute. They had just begun excavating Masada. Yigael Yadin, the chief archaeologist, gave a slide lecture to the scientific visitors, and I became instantly fascinated. On our return to the United States, I sent for the archaeological reports and read everything about Judea and Rome in those days. In the next several years, I wrote a novel called *Masada: The Last Fortress*, imagining life in the months of the siege. The manuscript went out to about eight publishers, all of whom praised its writing but rejected it for such reasons as "we don't do well with Jewish subjects." The book was finally published in 1998 by Eerdmans.

Your writing shows a deep concern with social issues. Is that related to your growing up Jewish?

I grew up in Brighton Beach, in Brooklyn, New York, an almost entirely Jewish neighborhood. My parents were not religious, however. In fact, my father went to work, as president of a shipping company, on Jewish holidays. Still, I grew up with the value system of my heritage, with the desire to *do good* and a strong social conscience.

Suicide is rarely thought to be an act of courage. Even during the Holocaust, it was not a common conscious decision. Yet, the suicide of the Jews at Masada is seen as courageous. Can you comment further on why this distinction is, or even should be, made?

During the writing of *Masada* I found myself struggling with the outcome chosen by the zealots. Could I bring myself to give up life for freedom?

I wrote a book about teenage suicide a long while ago, called *Close to the Edge*. In it a Jewish girl who has contemplated suicide befriends an old Jewish woman. She asks what makes life worth living. The woman says that even in the concentration camps the Jews held on though sick, starved, and miserable. They forced themselves to get through a day and then another and another—to spite the Germans. They believed that if they could survive the war they could live as human beings again. Sleep in a clean bed again. Hold their loved ones in their arms again. See that their torturers were punished!

The situation in Masada wasn't the same. They knew their fate if the Romans took the fortress. Death by the sword, or—if they became prisoners—death in the arenas or in the salt mines, or worse, a life of slavery. Their story tells the world that freedom is more important than life as a slave.

Biography ∽ GLORIA D. MIKLOWITZ

Gloria D. Miklowitz's forty-seven fiction and nonfiction books for children and young adults have won national and international awards and deal with important issues such as nuclear war, racial injustice, steroid abuse, date violence, and most recently, militia involvement. Recent books include *Masada: The Last Fortress* (winner of the 1998 Sugarman Family Award for Jewish Children's Literature), *Camouflage*, *Past Forgiving*, and *The Killing Boy*. Three of her novels were made into award-winning TV specials; *The War Between the Classes* won an Emmy for Best Children's Special in 1986. After graduating from the University of Michigan, Ms. Miklowitz became a script writer of documentary films on rockets and torpedoes, then turned to writing for children when her second son was born. A widow, Ms. Miklowitz lives in La Canada, California. Her two sons are college professors and her granddaughter is now writing picture books.

The Dead Man's Store

by Merrill Joan Gerber

People disappoint me, which is why I have started wearing black. There isn't one person I know who doesn't have a fatal flaw—and that includes my mother and father; my sisters, Franny and Erica; my present and past piano teachers, math teachers, and history teachers; and all my friends. The truth is that wearing black is my reminder to myself that people are impossible and there's pretty much no hope they'll ever understand me.

When Dad sees me come in carrying the newest black addition to my wardrobe, he groans and suggests that if I added a hat and a beard, I'd look just like a Hasidic rabbi. "You know we want you to be more Jewish, Rachel—but maybe you could learn to bake challah instead of shopping for clothes just like the ones you already have in your drawer. Do you intend to look like you're in mourning—instead of looking like the pretty *madele* you are?"

Maybe I do, I think to myself . . . *in mourning that you don't understand me, that you don't trust me to use my own judgment, that you won't give me some space to figure myself out before you want a signed* ketubah *on the wall.*

My mother doesn't have his reaction to my clothes, exactly, although she can't imagine why I've chosen such a dull "monotone" wardrobe. She fears she set me on the wrong track when once she gave me advice never to wear white or pastel pants: "One drop of chocolate ice cream, Rachel, one drop of spaghetti sauce, and that's the end of an expensive piece of clothing." She believes in total fabric protection: aprons over her dresses, couches covered with slipcovers, crocheted head rests on the two armchairs. She even put a plastic runner over the rug in the hallway; I can hear it squeaking right now as someone comes down the hall.

There's a knock on my bedroom door. This always poses a dilemma for me: If I say, "Yes?" and if it's one of my parents, they will always open the door and stick their head in. If I say, "What is it?" they will also open the door. Nothing I say is ever a signal for them *not* to open my door. Only my sister Franny, when she's home from Berkeley, has the good sense to make her request through the closed door because she is—as she tells me—"enlightened."

Now I try a new tack. "Just one minute, please . . . ," I say, but my mother replies, "It's only your mother," as she kicks open the door. A column of laundry marches in. "Here's your clean underwear, all washed and folded for Her Highness's convenience."

"I told you I was going to fold it; I told you to leave it in the basket."

"I can't wait that long," my mother says. "I only have a normal life span." She busies herself with the underwear. "I don't see any of your bras here, are you doing them by hand—those lacy ones?"

"I'm not wearing bras anymore. I threw all my bras away."

"You *what?* Is it all that radical stuff Franny is bringing home from Berkeley? Is she putting those feminine ideas into your head?"

"Feminist," I correct her. "Lacy bras are feminine. Throwing them out is feminist. But that's not what feminists do these days. They have advanced to more complicated agendas."

"Don't talk over my head, Rachel. Women—and you are a woman now—should not jiggle around all over the place."

"Bras bother me. They're tight. They push me up or squash me in—"

"The point is," my mother says, staring at me as if I am a moron, "you don't want boys looking at your body through your clothes."

"That is exactly why I wear black, Mom. No one can look through black unless he has X-ray vision. In fact, I need some new black things, so I'm biking over to The Bargain Buggy with Katya in a few minutes. There's a fantastic black Pendleton wool shirt I saw there the last time. I'm hoping it's still there and maybe on sale."

"Katya," my mother says grimly.

"What's wrong with Katya?" I ask.

Just at this moment my father comes down the hall.

"She's seeing Katya again," my mother says.

My father looks as if we've had some news about a serious medical condition from which I won't recover. "I feel I've failed you, Rachel," he says. "Your mother and I feel we have not given you a serious enough Jewish education. We worry that you don't have many Jewish activities. Or Jewish friends."

"Daddy, I have all *kinds* of friends. But of course I know I'm Jewish. I'm *glad* I'm Jewish. I enjoyed Sunday school when I was little. I even learned a lot from my Hebrew lessons. I could recite to you, right now, some verses from the Song of Solomon. I know more about being Jewish than you would believe, even if I didn't want to do the whole Bat Mitzvah thing. If you don't nag me all the time, I might even marry a Jewish boy."

"But you insist on going around with that German girl, you always tell us how much you like her brother—the one you said looks exactly like some actor you have a crush on. And you think it's perfectly okay that your sister Erica is engaged to Chris Scott—"

"Well, Erica loves Chris, Daddy. I know it's hard for you to accept a boy into the family whose name is Christian Scott, but after all—we live in the great melting pot of America, we're all mixed up together these days."

"But your friend, Katya—her great-grandfather was in the German army, Rachel. You told me so, yourself. A Nazi great-grandfather."

"Well, *my* great-grandfather was in the Russian army, wasn't he,

Daddy? I mean, what can we do about our great-grandfathers? Katya and I are not taking part in pogroms or killing anyone. We're just going to The Bargain Buggy to get some cheap clothes and save our parents tons of money we could be spending at the Fashion Mall."

"The Dead Man's Store," my mother intones. "You'll come home with leprosy one of these days. You don't know who was wearing those clothes, Rachel . . . or what diseases they had." She glances around my room as if it's decorated with dead rats. I have the feeling that one night she's going to tiptoe in and lower a termite tent over my head and then pump in poison gas to delouse me and all my clothes.

"I've really got to leave, Mom. Katya is waiting for me."

"What about her brother? Will he be there?" my father asks me.

"Karl? How could he be coming with us? He lives in Boston, Daddy. That's where he goes to college. We're going to the thrift shop five blocks from here, in *California*."

"Just as long as you're not planning to get involved with Katya's brother."

"Oh, Daddy, relax, please. You keep jumping way into the future. I want to get some clothes and you have me walking down the aisle. Why don't you bother Franny in Berkeley, call her up and tell her not to bring home some sweet bisexual boy?"

"Don't have a smart mouth, Rachel. If we'd raised you right, you would honor thy father and thy mother and not talk back."

"You did raise me right. You let me think for myself."

"Maybe we made a mistake," my father said.

"Just give me some space, Daddy. You might be surprised at how sensible I am."

Katya meets me on the corner of Orange Grove and we get right in synch on our bikes. Our hair blows in the wind and we ride side by side for a while till the traffic gets heavy. "Karl sends his regards," she yells from behind me. "He called home last night. He's got a girlfriend now. She's a math major."

But is she Jewish? I wonder. *German?* I worry that I'm beginning to think like my parents, as if the first thing you have to consider about a person is his religion or ethnic origin. I've always liked Karl, but he really isn't my type, though I like to let my parents worry. It could turn out that I *will* marry a German (if I marry at all) . . . or a Buddhist . . . or an African American—though I doubt it, given my deep down feelings. I could even marry a rabbi. Don't my parents realize we don't live in a *shtetl* in Poland, or even a Jewish neighborhood in Brooklyn like the one they came from? This is the melting pot of their dreams, the America my grandparents wanted for their children, and indirectly, my parents should realize, for me.

Katya squeals in delight when she sees that The Bargain Buggy has its belly-dance mannequin dressed in veils and coins outside the door. That means it's Stuff-Your-Bag day. We're really in luck: a whole bag full of clothes for five dollars. We lock our bikes around a light pole, stop to admire a big black motorcycle parked at the curb, and go inside.

"That smell," Katya says. She inhales, as if it's the rarest perfume, a combination of dust and wool and old leather and slightly worn-out clothes. We've agreed that the smell here is better than at the Fashion Mall, where there's a mixture in the air of chlorine and ammonia-sharp window cleaner and cheap plastic.

"I'm dying to find a red velvet cape," Katya says. "And a slinky satin evening gown."

"I'd like to buy that belly-dance costume on the mannequin," I tell her. "That would really give my father something to worry about; he'd start thinking I'm going to marry an Arab."

Katya and I each buy an empty paper bag from the woman at the front desk and fan out into the dream world of other people's lives, looking at and exclaiming over the bins of knickknacks, combs and wallets, costume jewelry, books and toasters, and real (if awful) oil paintings. On the New Arrivals table is a pink cashmere sweater (with just a few tiny moth holes) and it has a real mink collar. Not just a fur collar, but a collar made of the animal himself, a poor little mink who still has a head and eyes and sharp pointy teeth and a tail. Well, exotic as he is, I have a policy of not wearing real animals as clothing. I check out the stuffed animal bins (I used to have a Snoopy dog collection, but tired of it), the old purses, the antique cameras, the birdcages, the jigsaw puzzles. Katya is opening a paper parasol and twirling it over her head. We wave at each other and then—as I check out a rack of blue jeans (sometimes there are black jeans here)—I get a glimpse of an interesting person over in the Book Nook, my favorite part of the store. It's a cozy corner with a beanbag chair (leaking Styrofoam beads) and an overstuffed wing-back armchair.

Some guy is sitting in my favorite chair; he has a head of wild, unruly curls and a long, sensitive face. Something in his craggy features makes me think he might be Jewish. He's probably at least twenty years old, maybe even twenty-two. His long legs are stretched out and he's reading a tattered copy of *Zen and the Art of Motorcycle Maintenance*. My heart sinks when I see the black wool shirt draped over the arm of his chair with the Bargain Buggy price tag still on it. It's just the one I was hoping I'd still find here: the black Pendleton wool shirt with a silk lining. It's the very one I set my heart on when it was on the Ritz Rack where the really fancy stuff goes for five dollars and up—but now I can see it has a green label, which means it's been marked down as regular merchandise and like everything else in the store you can stuff it on Stuff-Your-Bag day. Nuts! This guy got to it first. And if I had arrived here just a few minutes earlier, I'd be wearing it to school every day next winter. I'm heartbroken. I hope it's full of holes. I can't help myself. I step over to the chair and actually lift up one black sleeve of it.

The guy looks up—he has blue eyes and a really kind expression when he says, "Oh, hi."

"Is this your shirt?" I say. "I mean, are you taking it?"

"I'm not sure," he says. "I'm considering it. It's got some moth holes in it."

"Oh, that's bad. They usually get much bigger. If there are still larvae in the wool, it'll turn into one major black hole."

"I guess I could wash it and scald the little guys," he says dubiously.

"You don't want to do that. Hot water will ruin wool."

"You seem to be quite an expert."

"I'm an expert on natural fibers, which is all I wear," I tell him. "And I only wear black," I add, though he surely didn't ask.

"Black is quite a statement," he says. "Quite a statement." He looks at me as if he really knows what I mean. Then he says, "Here, you take this shirt." He sort of holds it up against me. "I'm more the blue type. Blue jeans, blue work shirt, blue running shoes."

"Blue eyes," I say, and then I feel I went too far.

"Look, I'm really glad to let you have it. I wasn't that wild about it. And it probably isn't easy for you to find great black clothes. You look really good in black."

"Thank you."

Just then Katya comes swirling by in a red velvet cape and leopard skin boots. She's swinging a leather belt and looks a little like a lion tamer. "Look what I found!" she says. Then she sees my new friend and adds, "Look what *you* found."

"Joshua," he says, holding out his hand.

"Katya," she replies, shaking his.

"I'm Rachel," I say. I want her to go away and find some other lion to tame. Joshua takes my hand in his and holds it a second. "Great to meet you both. Do you come here often? I always come here," he says. "I get great novels for a quarter or fifty cents. Sometimes I find really cheap textbooks that cost fifty dollars at Cal State."

"You go to college?" Katya says. "We're still in high school." I give her a look—who asked her to explain our life histories?

"You ready to go soon?" Katya asks me. I realize I haven't even begun to fill up my bag, so I leave them and rush around the shop with my open paper bag and stuff in anything that's black and made of natural fibers—a black turtleneck sweater, black wool socks, black silk scarf, black leather belt. All the time I'm thinking of Joshua's blue eyes, though.

When my bag is bursting (I've added a man's black terry-cloth bathrobe) we all walk outside together.

"Are you a Zen Buddhist?" Katya asks, pointing to the book Joshua bought.

"Not exactly. I'm Jewish, in fact, but I'm interested in all that stuff. Sometimes I go up to the Buddhist monastery on Mount Baldy and spend a day, meditating. It's really peaceful up there, it puts things in perspective." He flings one of his long legs over the seat of his motorcycle.

"I'd like to learn about Buddhism," I say, out of the blue. "Maybe I could go with you sometimes."

"Sure, why not? Maybe we could meet here at The Bargain Buggy, same time next week, and then I'll ride you up there."

"Okay," I say. "I'll be here."

Katya kicks me. "You can't go on that thing without a helmet."

"I have an extra," Joshua says. "So see you then." Joshua revs up his motor. To be polite (I'm sure), he says to Katya, "And maybe I can take you for a ride someday, too." This time I kick Katya.

"No thanks," she says. "I like stretch limos."

And then he's gone in a blaze of noise and speed.

"You aren't really going up a mountain on a bike with a strange guy," Katya says to me. "You wouldn't!"

"Why not? My real life has to start somewhere."

"You don't even know who he is!"

"I'll get his last name. I'll get his license plate. Don't worry."

The wind is wild and sweet in our faces as we pedal home. There's so much ahead of me in life I can hardly wait to see what's in store. It's so strange that my parents want to foresee my exact fate and lock me into a future with all the labels stuck across my forehead: Educated (the right school), Employed (the right job), Married (the right boy— Jewish, of course). I wish they could see that I do appreciate their point of view, but they want it all settled in their minds right now when all I want is to take my time, to learn more about who I am and what I want.

I say good-bye to Katya at her house and ride on home. When I get in the door, my mother is waiting for me in the laundry room with her spot-remover spray bottle at the ready. She's got the washing machine filled with boiling hot water; my eyes tear up in the steam.

She pulls the bag out of my arms and says, "Right into the wash, young lady. God knows who wore those things and what's on them."

I wrench my treasures back from her arms and reach over to put the washer on "Spin." We stare at each other as the water whirls away in the centrifuge. "You can't wash wool or cotton in hot water, Mom," I tell her. "You're the one who taught me that. I'd have to be a pygmy to get into these things by the time you're done with them."

That's all I intend to say to her. She can only understand the practical level of life's problems, anyway. Eventually I hope my parents will figure out that they raised a mensch and be able to relax a little. I walk into my room and lovingly unpack my black clothes. The black terry-cloth bathrobe has the name of a French hotel embroidered over its pocket. It's very dramatic.

But then I take off all my clothes and put on the black Pendleton wool shirt. It's absolutely wonderful. The silk lining feels like a caress against my skin. I turn this way and that to see myself in the mirror. I like what I see, I'm taking shape under my clothing like a work of art.

Black is my banner these days. It's the backdrop to all my daydreams. I look in the mirror at the undecorated black of my shirt and see my future life painting itself on the fabric: flaming reds of freedom and revolt. Sweet, sad, dreamy violets and fuchsias of weeping and pain. The stark, cold ivory of loneliness. But, brighter and better than any of them, flaring on the canvas of my future, I see the blazing pinks of hope and love.

Interview ⌒ MERRILL JOAN GERBER

Tell us how you came to write "The Dead Man's Store."
The way a story comes into being is never perfectly clear: Many impressions form in advance of the moment I start to write. Related ideas at first seem to cluster aimlessly around a central core, like iron filings flying toward a magnet. Then, at a certain moment, an image forms, a clearer picture begins to develop, and I understand that I may begin to explore these ideas in a more specific way—on paper.

As the mother of three daughters growing up in a multiethnic environment, I was aware of the many attractions (and attractive men) that entered their spheres of experience. At some basic level, I found myself wanting them to choose Jewish men for their life partners, while at the same time recognizing that the voices of my aunts and grandmother and parents did not take into account the realities of the new world.

So your own experience growing up Jewish was different from your daughters'?
I grew up in a primarily Jewish world, first in Brooklyn, and then, during my high school years, in Miami Beach, Florida. The boys I knew were nearly all Jewish boys (in fact, I met my husband when I was fifteen and he, seventeen—though we didn't marry till seven years later). I never faced the challenges of dealing with the concerns of a mixed marriage, or even of falling in love with a non-Jewish boy.

Do you think being Jewish today is more complicated, then?
I think young people today are fortunate to be Jewish, with the freedoms long hoped for now a cherished reality for Jews (though it is in our nature to be forever afraid and thus forever vigilant). The idea that heaven is here on Earth and that we should live for ourselves and others, here and now, has a solid attraction for me, and places responsibility for love and commitment to others squarely on our shoulders.

In your story, Rachel seems both happily assimilated and confident in her own Jewishness—a difficult balancing act! Do you see this as a common combination?

Rachel's parents are more good-natured than strict, more full of banter and affection than of punitive threats and restrictions. Their protestations are serious, yet they know their limits. I think they basically trust their daughter (though they're sure it doesn't hurt to remind her of what they want, even if it's every ten minutes). "Go ahead and do what you want, but you'll break our hearts if you don't do what we want." That's a message that's still in force in families today, but I see that rational parents understand they can't live their children's lives. The few I know who have intransigent rules, which their children have broken in spite of many warnings, have suffered the terrible loss of their kids and their grandchildren. No expectations unfulfilled are worth losing contact with your children. Jews are still learning the meaning of "unconditional love"—a hard lesson to learn.

Biography ⌒ MERRILL JOAN GERBER

Merrill Joan Gerber has written nine novels for young adult readers, including *Handsome As Anything*, *I'd Rather Think About Robby*, and *Also Known As Sadzia! The Belly Dancer!*, along with novels, non-fiction, and short story collections for adults. Her stories have appeared in many prestigious magazines and journals, such as *The New Yorker*, *The Atlantic*, *Mademoiselle*, *Redbook*, *McCall's*, *and Ladies' Home Journal*. Among her many honors are the Prairie Schooners Reader's Choice Award, the Andrew Lytle Fiction Prize, the Best American Short Story Citation, and inclusion in *Prize Stories: The O. Henry Awards 1986* and *Best American Mystery Stories 1998*. The winner of a Wallace Stegner Fiction Fellowship to Stanford University, Ms. Gerber also holds an M.A. in English from Brandeis University. She lives in Sierra Madre, California, and teaches fiction writing at the California Institute of Technology.

Willow: A Passover Story

by Eric A. Kimmel

Passover comes out of a barrel.

Every spring, when leaves first appear on the rosebushes in our backyard, my grandmother starts emptying drawers and cupboards. She scrubs down every surface in the house. One morning, as if by magic, a barrel appears in the middle of the kitchen. Nana slowly lifts the lid. As if unearthing buried treasure, she takes out our Passover things and sets them carefully on the kitchen table.

Everything in that barrel is older than me. Some things are older than Nana. There's a set of silver cups that were given to my grandfather in 1923 when he was president of the Peczynizyn Fraternal and Benevolent Society. There's a stained, tattered matzo cover that a cousin made for my great-grandfather. The faded but beautifully embroidered Hebrew letters read: "To the upright and pious gentleman Reb Lazar Ya'akov Kerker—1888." There are meat dishes, chipped and cracked, with a blue and yellow cornflower pattern, and dairy dishes, which are plain white china. A heavy porcelain platter serves as our Seder plate. At last, emerging from the bottom of the barrel like Jonah's whale rising out of the sea, comes the silverware. These two sets of heavy, unadorned knives, forks, and spoons—solid and indestructible—look as if they've been in that barrel since the world began.

The meat set has a groove filed into the handle of each piece. The dairy set is plain.

I think my Uncle Al filed those grooves a long time ago. If he did, he was pretty smart, because that's the only way to tell the difference between the two sets. They look exactly alike, as if they came out of the same mold. Each piece has the word "Willow" engraved on its handle in deep letters that look as if they were pounded in with a sledgehammer.

In all the years we've been having Passover at our house, I never thought to ask why that word was there or what it meant. Most of the time I accept things the way they are. Especially with my grandmother in the house. Too many questions bring a pinch on the nose or a rap on the head with a thimble. But this year will be different. Now I'm old enough to understand that everything on the Passover table means something.

Why do we eat bitter herbs? Because the Egyptians embittered our ancestors' lives when they lived as slaves in Egypt. Why the salt water? To remind us of the tears our ancestors shed, and of the miracle at the Red Sea, when God split the waters. Why matzo? Because our ancestors left Egypt in such haste that their bread dough did not have time to rise. The tiniest details of the Seder table recreate miracles in which my own ancestors took part. This year, as my father reads the Haggadah, I am going to close my eyes and imagine that I am a Hebrew child living in Egypt on that holy night, with a pack on my back and sandals on my feet, listening to the wind-blown sand striking the house as God flies overhead, passing over the homes of the Israelites to smite the firstborn sons of the Egyptians.

And this year I am going to find out about Willow. What does the willow tree have to do with Passover? Why is the word "Willow" on all our silverware?

I ask Nana.

"What is 'willow'?" she asks in Yiddish.

"A *boimele*—a kind of tree," I tell her.

"I'll tell you about a tree," she begins. "There was a tree that grew in the forest near our farm in Galicia when I was a little girl. It was a tall, tall tree. Nobody had ever climbed to the top. Now, in those days I wasn't like you see me now, an old lady who can hardly walk, who creeps around like a spider. Back then I could run and climb. I could climb anything. I was the best climber of all, and I told all my friends that. So this one girl says to me—she was a Ukrainian girl, not a Jewish girl—if you're such a good climber, why don't you climb to the top of that big tree in the forest? I dare you to do it! So I did. I climbed right to the top. I climbed so high nobody on the ground could see me. And there I sat, right at the top of that tree, for hours and hours. It was magic. I could see all the way across the river, all the way to the mountains."

"What does that have to do with Passover?" I ask.

"Because this happened at Pesach. It was almost time for the Seder, and I still hadn't appeared. My parents were terrified. They thought I'd been carried off by a bear or evil spirits. My brother Yossel-Itzik finally found me and brought me home. Do you want to hear another story? This one's about a horse. You'll like it. There was a farmer near us who had a white horse . . ."

As much as I enjoy listening to my nana's stories, I eventually come to realize that she is not going to answer my question. Maybe she can't. Maybe she doesn't know what willows have to do with Passover.

I decide to ask someone who is sure to know: my Hebrew school teacher, Mr. Drori. Mr. Drori is a round, friendly man with a radiant smile. He was an Israeli. Anything or anyone from Israel—the Holy Land, the place where miracles happen every day—is extra special. I raise my hand after he takes roll and ask in a mixture of Hebrew and English, "*Mar Drori*, what is the connection between willow and Passover?"

Mr. Drori stares at me blankly. "Willow?" he asks. "*Mah zeh* 'willow'?"

My friend Daveed, who knows everything, pipes up with the word I wanted. "*Hadas*. Yitzhak wants to know what *hadas* has to do with

Pesach." We went by our Hebrew names in class. My full Hebrew name is Yitzhak-Eyzik Yehudah ben Moshe ha-Levi, or Yitzhak, for short. Daveed has it easy. He has the same name in Hebrew and English: David.

Mr. Drori thinks about the question. He thinks out loud. "Pesach. *Hadas. Hadas? Pesach?*" Finally he answers. "*Hadas* is one of the *arba minim*, the four species of plants that we use to make the *lulav*: the palm, the *etrog*, the myrtle, and the willow. But that is Sukkoth. Right now I can't think of any connection between willow and Passover." Then he smiles his beautiful smile. "But we won't give up. I will find out. I promise."

When I come to class next time, Mr. Drori isn't smiling. "Forgive me, Yitzhak. I tried my best. I asked all the other teachers, but no one seems to know of any connection between willow and Passover. I will keep trying. I will write a letter to my cousin who studies at a famous yeshiva in Jerusalem. He will ask the rabbis there. If there is an answer, they will surely know it. Unfortunately, I can't promise that you will have that answer by Pesach." It is already March, and Passover is only a few weeks away.

I am disappointed, but not heartbroken. If I don't find out this year, I will surely know the answer by next year. As I take my seat, the classroom door opens. Dr. Bruhl walks in. Dr. Bruhl teaches classes in Talmud and advanced Hebrew at the high school. He is a thin, pale man who speaks with a thick German accent. He always wears a suit and tie. In contrast to Mr. Drori, he never smiles.

"Forgive me for interrupting," he says to Mr. Drori. "I was told that one of your pupils asked about a connection between the willow tree and the Passover holiday."

"Yes. Yitzhak here wanted to know." Mr. Drori points to me. I sink down at my desk. To tell the truth, I am a little afraid of Dr. Bruhl. He hardly ever talks to elementary children.

Dr. Bruhl doesn't even look in my direction. He stands like a soldier at attention as he speaks to the whole class.

"I will explain the connection between Passover and the willow tree, or at least what it signifies to me. In 1944 I was in a concentration camp. I won't tell you what I experienced there; it was much, much worse than anything you can imagine. I was one of the lucky ones. The Germans didn't kill me right away, as they did so many others. Instead, I became a slave, like our ancestors in Egypt. They put me to work in a brick factory attached to the camp. I loaded bricks; I hauled bricks; I stacked bricks—thousands and thousands of them. It was brutal labor. They allowed us no rest. They beat us with whips. If a man fell under his burden, the guards shot him dead. Or kicked him to death with their boots. Our only food was a bowl of dirty water they called soup. Our clothes were rags. We slept four to a bunk without bedding or blankets of any kind. Many times I awoke to find myself sleeping between two corpses. The men beside me had died in the night.

"Our barracks were in the main camp. Every morning they marched us to the brickyard. A stream flowed by. Its water ran red from all the brick dust dumped into it. We called it "the bloody stream," because we used to say that it was our blood, the blood and life they sucked out of us to make those bricks, that made it run red. A willow tree grew beside the stream. We marched past it every day. The tree had no leaves. It stood dead and barren as everything else in that ghastly place. Willows grow near cemeteries, so we called it "the graveyard tree." We used to say that tree was growing on our graves, because the Germans dumped the ashes of the people they killed into that stream, too.

"One morning in early spring, as we marched through the mud beside the stream, I noticed green speckles covering the willow's branches. The tree, which we all assumed to be dead, had burst into bloom. 'Look, Comrades!' we whispered to one another as we passed. 'The graveyard tree is blooming! There *is* life in this desert. God has not forsaken us. He will free us from Hitler as he freed our ancestors from Pharaoh.' Three weeks later a Russian tank broke down the gates of the camp, the guards ran away, and we were free.

"And that, at least to me, is the connection between willows and Passover. A willow tree grows in a park not far from my house. I always cut a few branches for my Seder table. I hope that answers the question." Dr. Bruhl nods to Mr. Drori. He leaves, closing the door behind him.

No one says anything after that. Mr. Drori goes over the weekly Torah portion. Then he tells us some funny stories about his experiences in the Israeli army. Nobody feels like laughing. Not even Mr. Drori.

I remember what Dr. Bruhl told us. At our Seder a few weeks later, when my father finishes reading the part in the Haggadah about the Pesach sacrifice, the matzo, and the bitter herbs, I suddenly announce, "I know why our Passover silverware says 'Willow.'"

Everybody stares at me. "Why?" my mother asks. So I proceed to tell everyone at the table—my parents, Nana, my younger brother, Jonny, my uncle Al, and my aunt Jenny—the story that Dr. Bruhl told our Hebrew school class.

"That's a beautiful story," my mother says when I finish.

Aunt Jenny translates my story into Yiddish. She sounds like Betty Boop, no matter which language she's speaking.

"*Zehr shayn, zehr shayn,*" Nana agrees. Uncle Al gives me a wink. "Pretty good, kiddo! How'd you like to hear another story about willows and Passover?"

"Okay," I reply. Uncle Al has a bar on Canal Street. He knows lots of good stories, mostly about his friends who grew up to become gangsters.

Here's what my uncle tells me:

"Years ago, when your mother and I were kids, we lived in a nice little apartment on Chrystie Street in Williamsburg. Every year I'd help my father haul the Passover barrel—the same barrel that's in your basement—up from the cellar so that Nana could get everything ready for the Seder. For years, the silverware we used at Passover was some ugly, cheap stuff someone must have picked up from a pushcart when they first came to America. Nothing matched. The forks and spoons were rusty, stained, bent; you could scrub and scrub with steel wool, but they never came clean. One year Nana got sick of it. 'Alfred,' she said to me, 'can't you find some decent Passover silverware? I hate this shabby junk. I'm ashamed to put it on the table.'

"'Leave it to me, Ma!' I said. 'I'll find some silverware for you. I know just the place.'" Uncle Al pauses. I glance around the table. My father is listening with great interest; my brother has fallen asleep; Nana is studying her Haggadah; my mother looks stern; and Aunt Jenny's bracelets jingle as she tries to keep from laughing. "So, Al? Tell us the rest," she says in perfect Betty Boop.

"What happened? Where did you find the silverware?" I ask.

"Figure it out, sport," says Uncle Al, flashing a wise-guy grin. "We lived across the street from the Willow Cafeteria."

Interview ⁓ ERIC A. KIMMEL

The diligent search for meaning in your story, even between
seemingly unconnected words such as "Passover" and "Willow,"
is reminiscent of Torah study. Yet, in this case, the search comes
to a lighthearted conclusion. Can you comment on the combination
of seriousness and humor?

When you study Torah commentaries, you discover that there are simple explanations and more complicated, even far-fetched ones, to answer the same question. Which is correct? They both are, depending on what you learn from each. Is "Willow" a grim Holocaust story, or is it a funny American story? Maybe it's both, just as we are both Jews and Americans.

Your own grandmother was a great storyteller. Is she Nana in
"Willow"?

"Willow" is a true story. My uncle Al stole the Passover silverware from the Willow Cafeteria. My family used that same set for forty years. My grandmother, who was extremely pious, conveniently chose to ignore the fact that her Pesach silverware was stolen goods.

Dr. Bruhl and Mr. Drori were my teachers at the East Midwood Jewish Center. I described them both as I fondly remember them. Dr. Bruhl's story was inspired by my friend Mayer Zar, who was a slave laborer in several concentration camps. Mayer's experience was ghastly. You can read about some of it in a book entitled *In the Mouth of the Wolf*, written by his wife, Rose. Despite what he went through, Mayer has a great sense of humor. He is the type of person who can fix or build anything. I asked him where he learned all his skills. He replied, "You see, Eric, in my younger days I was enrolled in a work-study program . . . under the Germans."

And Uncle Al's friends really grew up to be gangsters?

Uncle Al wasn't actually a gangster, but plenty of his friends were. He grew up with people named Bugsy, Meyer, and Lepke. Uncle Al was a very tough customer. But he had his good side. He never turned his back when someone was bad-mouthing Jews or pushing around a Jewish person. Anti-Semites usually made a quick trip to the hospital when Uncle Al was around. He taught me to be proud to be Jewish, never to be afraid of anti-Semites, and that we don't have to like people who hate us. Learn to defend yourself. I think this is still good advice for Jewish children today.

Any other advice you'd like to pass on?
I love being Jewish. It's a privilege to be Jewish. It's also a privilege to be African American, Native American, Latino, Vietnamese, Appalachian, East Coast Aristocrat, or what have you. Take pride in who you are and what you are. Know where your family comes from and how you came to be the person who lives inside your skin. Don't be a doormat, and don't look for scapegoats. Never, never put down people who are different. Stereotypes are lies and people who believe them are fools. The experience of every group is valuable. But don't get so locked into your own group that you forget the larger picture. We are all Americans, citizens of a great country that takes our differences and makes them its strength. We are all human beings, citizens of the world. Every human being is part of our family.

Biography ∽ ERIC A. KIMMEL

Eric A. Kimmel grew up in Brooklyn, New York, and remembers going to Ebbetts Field to see the Dodgers play. He also remembers always wanting to be a writer, "maybe even before I knew how to write." Along with his education at the East Midwood Jewish Center, he learned about traditional Eastern European culture firsthand from his grandmother, "a terrific storyteller." Mr. Kimmel's books have won numerous awards, among them a Caldecott Honor Medal for *Hershel and the Hanukkah Goblins*, the Sydney Taylor Award from the Association of Jewish Libraries for *The Chanukkah Guest*, and a Texas Bluebonnet Award nomination for *The Adventures of Hershel of Ostropol*. Other titles on Jewish themes include *Be Not Far from Me: Legends from the Bible* and *Bar Mitzvah*. "I love to write funny stories," he says, "especially Jewish ones. Jewish literature has a vast tradition of humor. We could not have survived our misfortunes without the ability to laugh at ourselves, and at our oppressors."

Fly Me to the Moon

by Sonia Levitin

Drew-David's mother kissed him quickly, giving him a slight push on the shoulder. He looked away, afraid he might falter. "I'll miss you," he whispered.

"We'll miss you, too, terribly." His mother dabbed her eyes. "Use the tele-com all you want, don't worry about the cost."

"Let your mother know you're all right," said his father, trying to smile but looking worried. "Of course, Mission Control will inform us of your safe landing, but it's the little things—keep us posted. And, of course, we'll fly out to visit as soon as we can."

Drew-David sank down into the sculpted seat and strapped himself into the capsule, one of six hundred that lined the rocket on either side. Wide windows in the ceiling of the craft would afford a view of the galaxy, whirling stars, and a panoply of colors. However, Drew-David could not see any of the other young colonists who, like himself, had undergone a long and strenuous selection process.

He had been surprised at the lack of orientation. Of course, he was given tapes about climate control, weightlessness, food, and protective clothing. Even his father, who usually did not comment on decisions made by the Council, seemed perplexed. "Didn't they tell you kids anything about organization? I mean . . ."—he coughed his nervous little cough—"like who's in charge and how to go about—you know—organizing yourselves into a real colony, a community?"

"No," said Drew-David. "I guess they'll tell us when we get there. I'm sure the Council will send some leaders with us."

"Perhaps, they want you young people to create your own society," said his mother, reaching into the Auto-Prep for their dessert—chocolate cake for Dad, lemon pie for Drew-David, and a Nutra Crunch bar for herself. "They did a similar thing with those people they sent into orbit a few years ago. Remember?"

Drew-David's father grunted loudly. "Who can forget? Three of them never came back. Killed one other. I don't know. I don't like the idea of this, but you two—"

"Whomever the Council selects," Drew-David's mother said sternly, "is not only honored but obligated."

"I want to go!" Drew-David had called out, for the first time acknowledging the depth of his yearning to leave Earth and all its tight little groups and procedures. He had never really fit in with his age-mates. As a colonist, perhaps, he would no longer be an outsider. He had prayed each night for this, sitting in his round chamber, looking out at the sky. "Fly me to the moon!" he had implored, imagining some presence there beyond the clouds and the stars. "Please, let me go."

Now through the rocket came a blast of sound, then precise orders. "Buckle straps, everyone. Number 12, please buckle up. Number 442, please activate your oxygen tank located in the panel in front of you . . ."

Directions continued to individual travelers, and Drew-David was gratified to notice that all the system lights in his small compartment were lit and the printout on his screen said, SYSTEMS GO. RELAX, HAVE A GOOD FLIGHT.

There was the rattle and boom of acceleration, the mighty outward thrust, then the sudden calm, a floating sensation, accompanied by a faint mist that wafted through the capsule, inducing relaxation and sleep.

And while he slept, Drew-David half thought and half dreamed of how he would now belong, a colonist among other settlers. He wondered which of the age-mates from his quadrant would be here with him. Probably Alain, and Orson, Liz, Madison, and Matt—they were the popular kids, the planners, bound for political life and leadership, you could tell. They were the beautiful, accomplished ones, the sort that made him feel shrunken and inept.

A dark notion intruded on his reverie, causing him to wake up with a jolt. Why had they chosen him? He had no particular talent or distinction. Why was he chosen?

Drew-David let out a gasp. He was the only Jew in his quadrant; in fact, the only Jew in his entire form. His parents were cheerfully unreligious, Jews mainly by definition and a few odd habits. They shrugged at his reading of history and theology, smiled at his esoteric knowledge of ancient rituals. They accepted Drew-David as a thoughtful child who for some reason unknown to them liked digging into his cultural genesis. All right. He was a good son, a fine student; they didn't expect to understand him.

It struck him suddenly that maybe this "contest" was a ruse. Drew-David began to tremble as he thought back to historical accounts of persecutions and pogroms. Such things, of course, no longer existed. Since the advent of the International Ministries, aggressive actions were instantly punished. But . . . something in memory, ancient, collective memory, filled Drew-David with anxiety. Wasn't it a truism that the Jews, as soon as they became complacent, were once again singled out for destruction? It would be relatively simple to gather them up by inventing a contest of sorts, some excuse to launch them not to the moon, but to outer space, and then simply let them go, let them spin themselves into oblivion in the dark reaches of space.

Ridiculous! responded his more rational self. Think of the numbers involved! *Anything is possible,* he countered; in this electronic age, why, the mere tap of a few keys could collect thousands, millions of people and send them anywhere. Perhaps this rocket was just one of hundreds, a fleet designed to solve the "Jewish Question" once and for all.

His stomach rumbled. His forehead felt damp. Drew-David reached for the Paci-cone and placed the tube over his mouth and nose, inhaling deeply of the sweet, soothing mist that set him again to dreaming.

Melodies flooded into the capsule; various colors and brilliances showed through the windows above. Then came the voice: "Welcome to the moon. It is an auspicious moment, as you, the chosen emissaries of the best that is on Earth, have arrived to found a new nation here, a nation that exemplifies all that is good and lasting and vital to survival."

The message was repeated several times as the doors of the craft slid open.

Drew-David unbuckled his harness, pulled down his helmet, took his possessions, and stepped out onto lunar soil. He lifted one foot, then the other, and felt himself glide slowly over a mound of craggy stones.

All around him other young people were leaping, dancing their moon walks, eyes wide and round inside their bubble helmets, mouths open in amazement and delight.

Through speakers in their helmets, the voice summoned them to form a circle. Drew-David moved with the others, searching for a familiar face, finding none. He felt an instant of panic.

A whir of sound, and swiftly a transparent dome was raised over them. The speaker instructed them to remove their outer gear and their helmets. "You will find the atmosphere quite comfortable. You will breathe normally; you will be held by gravity, just as on Earth."

Drew-David gazed at the others, and he saw a mix of people that had obviously been carefully planned. All colors, races, bodily shapes and sizes, all postures and attitudes were represented here. And now, as they stood in a large circle, the speaker addressed them.

"You have come to colonize this sphere where there has never been strife or animosity or any violence, except that which nature decrees. Who should be chosen for such a mission? We have spent many years deliberating this question, and at last the Council came to a unanimous conclusion, that what is needed is not uniformity, but its opposite. Diversity."

Drew-David gazed at the people all around him. Now he could see in the set of their faces and their bodies a certain shared determination and sense of self. Not one of these youths was the sort to follow the crowd or to subjugate others. They were individualists. As Drew-David pondered this, the speaker continued.

"You, the first six hundred young colonists, embody all our cherished hopes. Each of you has a special and unique disposition and ability. Each of you is needed here."

In the next moment there was silence. The six hundred people stood in the circle, reluctant to break out, waiting for instructions. Soon it became clear that now there would be no instructions. People began to smile, to swing their arms, shuffle their feet, to speak to those around them.

Drew-David turned to the girl beside him. She wore her long hair in braids, and her skin was flawless without makeup or any artificial beauty marks, such as were currently popular. "Hi," he said shyly. "I'm Drew-David. Where are you from?"

"I'm Reana, from North East Triad," she said. "I don't know why I was chosen. Of course, I was eager to come. I couldn't wait for the selection."

"What did you do while you waited?" Drew-David asked.

She smiled. "I guess I did what I always do. After school I'd go out to the woods and play." She laughed slightly. "None of my friends can understand it. They think I'm off circuit."

"Play." Drew-David laughed slightly. "What did you play with?"

"My violin. I know I'm old-fashioned, but I still love the music that a real violin makes. I have a very old instrument. It was made centuries ago. It's here, among my things."

"Show me," said Drew-David.

The girl found her luggage and the violin case. She opened the fasteners and lifted up her violin, caressing it with her eyes for a moment before she placed it beneath her chin. She drew the bow across the strings, and the small space between them was suddenly filled with beautiful music.

Now, all around him, Drew-David noticed the others talking, and he heard bits of conversation, saw cherished possessions being brought out and shared, every kind of treasure imaginable—microscopes, ballet shoes, paints and brushes, musical instruments, recording devices, tools and equipment for sports and inventions, sacks full of seed and saplings to create new growing things here on the moon.

Small groups formed as people showed their treasures and exchanged their ideas. Their future would contain concert halls, gardens and primeval forests, lakes, beautiful structures, conservatories, stadiums, canteens where food was wholesome and delicious, available to everyone. Indeed, they were planning a virtual paradise here on the moon.

Now names were called by the unseen speaker, and one by one a bright beam shone upon the person summoned—an inventor of a new light source, a young agronomist, a breeder and healer of animals, an astronomer, all with their instruments and their expertise.

Drew-David was entranced, listening and watching, looking from one to the other of these talented, extraordinary people. He recalled the welcoming words—"all that is good and lasting and vital to survival." He felt a wave of gratitude and awe, then a moment of consternation. What was he doing here? What was his role?

He heard his name booming from the speaker, the echoes settling around him: "Drew-David! Drew-David! Step forward, please!"

Thrust into the glaring spotlight, Drew-David felt a rising panic. What must he do? He was a fraud, devoid of any new ideas or brilliant abilities. He looked out into the cosmos at the glittering stars and black velvet darkness surrounding them. He felt a chill running across his back, a deep and terrible yearning. And then he knew, with certainty and exultation.

Drew-David reached into his duffel bag, rummaging inside for the objects he had packed without clear thought, but in a burst of emotion.

He found them, two slender candles, two small brass holders, and a pack of matches.

Drew-David set the candles upon a stone, tall and flat topped, like a small altar.

Silence settled inside the dome, a hush that drew all the six hundred together as if tied by silken cords.

Drew-David struck the match. He lit first one candle, then the other. He lifted his hands over the two small flames, and in clear, resonant tones, he said the prayer of thanksgiving that Jews have given throughout the ages.

"Blessed are You, Lord our God, King of the universe, who has granted us life, sustained us and enabled us to reach this occasion."

When he was finished, Drew-David looked about at the people who encircled him. Every face held a radiance, which Drew-David knew must also be reflected in his own. And it was good.

Interview ⌒ SONIA LEVITIN

In spite of the futuristic setting of your story, in which Drew-David's parents are "cheerfully unreligious," he and his family are still "Jews . . . by definition" and Drew-David is still drawn to the "ancient rituals" and fearful of persecution. Do you see parallels in our own time?

Yes, I do see parallels between Drew-David's family and our own time. Today, many people seem estranged from their religious roots. Some long for a closer connection with God. My novel, *The Singing Mountain*, deals with that very theme. In "Fly Me to the Moon," Drew-David worries about being different from his classmates and his parents, delving into spiritual matters. So it is for many of us today. Being "different" arouses anxiety and fear of not being accepted. But in the long run, that very difference can lead to the greatest fulfillment and, ultimately, not only acceptance but real understanding.

Science fiction is a new departure for your writing, isn't it?

I suppose I've been in a "sci-fi" mode since I just finished my latest book, *The Cure*, which combines science fiction and a terrifying incident from the middle ages. In that book, people are ruled by a dictatorial government that forbids all diversity, art, self-expression. My fervent hope is that before long we will come to value our diversity, encouraging individual differences, letting each person's creativity add value and enlightenment to the community. So, what I have created in this story is really a dream and a wish of how the world might yet be. I asked myself what it is that Jews offer the world. I think it is a sense of holiness, from which all morality stems.

Much of your writing has been on Jewish topics. Did you grow up in a traditionally observant family?

No. When I was four years old, my family escaped from Germany just before World War II. We were very lucky, as many in my extended family did not leave and were killed. I have always been aware of the fact that being alive is a privilege. I grew up in Los Angeles, the only Jewish child in my grammar school. I felt somehow obligated to explain Judaism to my friends. They were so startled that we did not keep Christmas or Easter. I remember their astonished looks, amazement and, almost, pity. Still, I did have many friends, and I always thought it was important to stress our similarities, not our differences.

When I began writing, I did not want to be classified as a "Jewish writer," because I wanted to speak to all people, not only my coreligionists. I soon discovered that some of my best writing came from my own Jewish roots. I remember going to synagogue with my parents on festivals and High Holy Days. I especially loved the solemnity, the chants and songs, and being close to my family. We always lit candles on Friday night, but as the years went on, the other rituals decreased. Only in the last ten years have we—my husband and I—become truly observant. Now I see our tradition as a great treasure.

Biography ⟶ SONIA LEVITIN

Sonia Levitin was born in Berlin, Germany, and at the age of four escaped with her mother and sisters to the United States. Her first book, *Journey to America*, is based on that experience, with *Silver Days* and *Annie's Promise* continuing the fictionalized autobiography. The author of more than thirty books for young readers in a variety of genres, Ms. Levitin has been honored with the National Jewish Book Award, Edgar Award, Western Writer's Silver Spur Award, Sydney Taylor Award, PEN Award, Austrian Book Prize, and German Bishop's Award, among many others. Her books of Jewish interest include the novels *The Return*, *The Golem and the Dragon Girl*, *Escape from Egypt*, and *The Singing Mountain*. Ms. Levitin began her career as a junior high school teacher and has continued in teaching as an instructor of creative writing for UCLA Extension. She is the mother of a grown son and daughter, Daniel and Shari. She and her husband live in southern California.

Family History

by Johanna Hurwitz

Yesterday I had softball tryouts after school and so I cut my Bar Mitz-vah class.

I was glad I had a good excuse, but the truth is, I probably would have skipped class without an excuse, too. It's hard enough to spend a full day in school, doing geometry and science, reading *Julius Caesar* in English and smelling spring outside the window. Who wants to go from one classroom to another, from junior high to the synagogue building?

The softball tryouts went very well and the coach said I would def-initely make the cut for the team this season. For supper, Mom had cooked chicken my favorite way and so I was feeling really great when the phone rang. "It's for you, Charlie," Mom said.

Of all people, it was the cantor. Before I could even explain any-thing to him, he said, "Get your haftorah. We'll rehearse you over the phone."

Can you imagine? There I was digesting chicken and chanting my lines over the kitchen phone.

"Look what technology has brought us to," my father said when I hung up. "For centuries boys went and studied in schoolrooms. And now, you can learn your *aleph bet* via telephone."

I thought I was lucky that he was so amused by my modern lesson that he forgot to ask why I hadn't worked with the cantor during the afternoon. But he must have guessed something because while I was up in my bedroom, doing my geometry homework, Dad came and knocked on my door. "So, how's it going?" he asked when he came in and sat down on my bed.

"Geometry isn't that hard," I said, shrugging my shoulders.

"Not geometry," he replied. "I mean your Bar Mitzvah studies. June isn't so far off, you know."

"I know," I said. My stomach, filled with Mom's chicken, gave a lurch. It's the way I always feel when I think about getting up before the whole congregation and all my relatives and friends and chanting the Torah portion and then my haftorah.

"Why do I have to do it?" I blurted out. "I don't even believe in all this stuff."

"It's not the *stuff* that matters," my father said. "It's the tradition. The continuity of a line going back and back." He paused a moment and removed some typed pages from an envelope that he was holding.

"If you don't have too much homework, I thought you might want to read this. I'd put it away so carefully that I only just found it again."

"What is it?" I asked grumpily. Wasn't it enough that I had homework and Hebrew studies? Now he wanted me to read something else.

"My grandfather, your great-grandfather, wrote some of his memories down in Yiddish. And my father translated them so I could read them. Now I think you should read them, too."

I looked at the yellowing sheets that my father held. "How old are they?" I asked.

"These memories are over a hundred years old. It's history. Family history."

I admit I was a little curious.

When my father left the room, I shoved my math aside and began reading.

I was seven years old when my papa died. It was February and the weather was cold. My father's death was so terrible that for days I couldn't stop shivering. But I wasn't shivering from the weather. It was the coldness inside me, not outside, that made my body shake.

I cried and cried. I loved Papa very much and the thought that I would never see his face or hear his voice again was more than I could bear. I wished that I could die, too, so that we could once again be together.

Of course, my mama was sad, too. But being a mother, she had work to do. She still had to clean the house, do the laundry, and cook meals for her four children: my sister, Anna, who was nine, and my little brothers, Ely, who was four, and Saul, who was only two.

I went to school, but I didn't study. I sat in the classroom and I didn't hear a word the teacher said. I didn't eat the lunch that my mother packed for me, and I didn't eat my meals at home. Food had no taste. And besides, if I wanted to die then the quickest way to do that was to starve myself to death. Sometimes I cheated and I took a swallow or two of water. I ate a bite or two off the crusts of bread, but I didn't eat any meat. And I wasn't tempted by the cakes that our neighbors brought.

My mother begged me to eat. But nothing she said made any difference. Then she asked the rabbi to speak to me. "Chaim," he said, "you must eat. It is very important that you don't get sick."

"I don't care," I told him.

"But I have a secret to tell you. I know you miss your father. But I have good news."

"What good news?" I asked.

The rabbi scratched his big black beard and smiled at me. "Your father is going to return to you."

"He is? When?" I asked, amazed at this wonderful news.

"He will come at Pesach. He will be at the door when you open it for Elijah."

I could not contain my joy. "Does my mother know?" I

asked the rabbi. I knew she would be just as happy as I was.

"No. No," the rabbi said. "And you mustn't say a word about this. I told you it was a secret. Don't tell anyone. Just be patient. And in the meantime, eat, study, and do all the things your father would want you to do."

"Can't I even tell Anna?" I asked. I knew she'd be so happy to hear this good news, too.

"No. You must tell no one," the rabbi insisted.

It was such a big secret that I thought I would burst. Everyone must have been amazed that suddenly I could smile and laugh again. I cleaned my plate and even ate the scraps that my little brothers left from their meals. My appetite was enormous, as if making up for the meals I had missed.

They tell me that from February till mid-April, when the Pesach holiday began, I grew two inches and gained many pounds. It was true. Suddenly, all my clothes became too small and my mother was kept busy making clothing for me. She cut up a pair of my father's old pants, and I almost blurted out my secret. If she cut up his clothing, what would my father wear when he returned? But just in time, I remembered my promise to the rabbi and I held my tongue.

Finally, it was the evening of the first Seder. The house was cleaned of all *chametz*, and my mother had made a huge pot of chicken soup. There was a roast chicken and vegetables all cooked and ready. My brothers and Anna and I sat around the table, shining with cleanliness. The Haggadah was open before us, and the Seder plate with its shank bone and bitter herbs was in the center of the table as the meal began.

"Why is this night different from all other nights?" Only I knew why as I waited impatiently for that moment when we would open the door.

And then the most terrible thing happened. When it was finally time to look for Elijah, the moment I had been waiting and waiting for, I jumped up and threw the door open. And just like the year before and the year before that, no one was there. Not Elijah and not my father.

I let out such a scream of disappointment and rage. I am sure they heard me throughout our town and in the next town, too.

"Hush, hush," my mother said in amazement and ignorance. "Perhaps Elijah will come next year."

At that moment, I stopped believing in God. I no longer attended the Hebrew school. I wouldn't speak to the rabbi. It was as if I became a different person. Two years later, my mother's older brother, my uncle Yankel, sent enough money for us all to go to America.

I became an American boy, studying English, learning everything about my new country. And I never went to the synagogue.

But one year, many, many years later, I remember it was in April, around the time of Pesach, when I was a grown man with a wife and children of my own, I happened to look in the mirror and was stunned to see my father's face.

It is true that when I was young people had said that I, more than my brothers, resembled my father. But I had never agreed. Suddenly, I could see it. There were my father's eyes looking out at me from the mirror. In a way, it was as if he had returned.

My wife was amazed when I suggested that maybe we should hold a Seder that year. Every year before, I had refused. I hadn't even liked going to the Seders given by her family.

"All at once you have religion?" she said to me.

"No," I said. "It's hard to explain." But suddenly, I was a link to the past. How could I say that my father had returned. That I was my father. And someday my son would be me. That we were part of a chain that would never be broken, no matter what happened.

I realize now that the rabbi who lied to me about my

father's return was not the evil man I had considered him to be for so many years. He was ignorant. In his bumbling way he tried to get a little boy to eat his supper. To smile and play again. And to continue to grow up. In that, he succeeded.

I am my father's son. And you are mine. And I know I won't see my father again or the children of my children's children. But we are linked together. And somehow, that makes me feel good.

When I finished reading the yellowed sheets, I took out my haftorah pages and read them through again. I chanted the words quietly to myself and I only stumbled once. By June when I become a Bar Mitzvah, I know I'll ace my portion. My parents won't have to worry about me embarrassing them. I'm sorry that I never knew my great-grandfather. I wish he could be here, but my grandfather is coming from Florida. It's kind of neat to think that I'm a link in that chain that goes back and back and back. It makes me feel good.

Interview ⌒ JOHANNA HURWITZ

What can you tell us about the background of "Family History"?
The idea for "Family History" is actually just that. The father-in-law of a cousin told me about his childhood and how he had been affected by the death of his father. As in my story, the *shtetl* rabbi tried to assuage the grief by telling the boy that his father would return at Pesach with Elijah. I was moved by this tale and never forgot our conversation.

How much of your writing comes from your own experiences growing up Jewish?
Unfortunately for me, I did not grow up Jewish. My parents were modern, assimilated Jews. We celebrated no holidays and never attended synagogue. Even my name was ambiguous. My last name was Frank and during my school years I met other students with the same last name who were Christian. I wrote about the emptiness and confusion I felt from my lack of religion in my book *Once I Was a Plum Tree*.

As an adult, I began to discover my Jewish roots through literature. I read the works of Sholem Aleichem, Mendel Mocher Seforim, Isaac Bashevis Singer, and others. I was about to enroll in a Yiddish class when I met my future husband. He had been born in Berlin but had grown up in Palestine/Israel. Instead of Yiddish, I began to study Hebrew. I never succeeded in mastering Hebrew, but from my husband I learned much about Jewish history and about the founding of the State of Israel.

My maternal grandfather was a rabbi and died when my mother was twelve years old. Her family with seven daughters grew away from their religion. However, listening to my mother's stories from her childhood, and using poetic license, I reconstructed some of her youth in my book *The Rabbi's Girls*. By writing that book, I felt closer to the grandfather I had never known and recaptured some of my own family history.

In "Family History," the father remarks, "It's not the stuff that

*matters. It's the tradition." There are those who would argue
"Why carry on a tradition whose 'stuff' doesn't matter?" What is
it about Judaism, do you think, that allows for tradition to outlive
even faith?*

The rabbis tell us that we need not believe to carry on as Jews. Observance of traditions binds us as a tribe. It roots us to a heritage dating
back thousands of years and gives continuity to our existence. On a
Saturday morning when Jews in New York sit in a synagogue and read
the Torah portion of the day, that same portion is read in synagogues
throughout the country and (taking into account the time differences)
throughout the world. Similarly, when Jews and their friends sit at the
Seder table, they are joined in spirit with Jews throughout the world.

My story is about continuity and its importance. My father never
became a Bar Mitzvah, nor did my brother. However, when my children were thirteen, they each stood before the ark and recited their
Torah portion and haftorah. "This proves," I told the rabbi, "that a
broken chain can be mended."

Does the chain connect Jews to others as well?

The Jewish heritage is one that is enjoyed and shared by Jews and non-
Jews alike. The concept of a single God and the values in the Ten
Commandments are crucial to our culture. Compassion, concern for
the elderly, aid to the impoverished, and sharing of wealth are all Jewish values that have helped mankind.

The Jewish respect for education and learning has resulted in great
thinkers and major contributions in all fields: the sciences, philosophy,
and literature. Jewish youngsters should feel pride in their heritage. But
just as all people gain from Jewish contributions, we all gain from other
cultures as well. It is important to learn about one another and gain
understanding and appreciation of our differences. This is one of the
themes of my book *Faraway Summer.*

Biography ∽ JOHANNA HURWITZ

The author of more than fifty books for young readers, Johanna Hurwitz grew up in the Bronx, near enough to Yankee Stadium that she could hear the cheering whenever someone hit a home run. A graduate of Queens College, with a master of library science degree from Columbia University, she was a children's librarian in public and school libraries for many years. Her books include *The Adventures of Ali Baba Bernstein, Baseball Fever, Class Clown,* and *Russell Sprouts,* along with titles of particular Jewish content: *Once I Was a Plum Tree, The Rabbi's Girls, Faraway Summer,* and biographies of Anne Frank and Leonard Bernstein. Among her honors are children's choice awards in Texas, Mississippi, West Virginia, South Carolina, Florida, New Jersey, Wyoming, and Kentucky; the Weekly Reader Book Club Award; the Parents Choice Award; and several American Library Association Notable Books of the Year. Ms. Hurwitz is married, the mother of two grown children, and the grandmother of Ethan. She divides her time between Great Neck, New York, and Wilmington, Vermont.

Cain and Abel Double-Date

by Susan Beth Pfeffer

His parents were arguing again. Cain couldn't remember a time when they got along. This time their fight was about clothes.

"You got us thrown out just so you could wear clothes," Adam was saying. "Admit it, Eve. It was dresses you were after all along."

"I don't see you in a fig-leaf apron," Eve replied.

"Come on," Cain's brother, Abel, said. "You're both great dressers and you know it."

Abel must have done something, because first Eve laughed, and then Adam. Cain smiled without even knowing what Abel had pulled off this time. It just made him feel better when his parents weren't yelling, and Abel alone had the knack for making them laugh.

"Hey, Cain!" Abel shouted. "We have big plans for this evening."

"Coming," Cain said. He was still confused about this date business. "We eat dates," he'd said to Abel when the subject first came up that morning. "Do you mean we're supposed to share one date with two girls?"

"You're right, big guy," Abel had replied. "A date is a fruit, and we eat plenty of them. But a date also means spending some time with a pretty girl. Or in this case, two pretty girls. Tiffany for me and Amber for you."

"But how can *date* mean two different things?" Cain had asked. He was older than Abel, but Abel was smarter, and always seemed to know things Cain couldn't guess at.

"There just aren't enough words for all the different things around," Abel said. "So sometimes a word has to have two different meanings. Blame it on progress."

Cain wasn't sure what progress was, but decided not to ask. Amber and Tiffany were pretty girls. They'd moved into the neighborhood just a few days before, and Abel had wasted no time getting to know them. Cain was glad there were two of them, since they were the only girls he'd ever seen.

"You look great," Abel said as Cain joined him in front of the tent. "Amber is bound to go for you big time."

Cain blushed. Abel was a lot better looking than he was, and much better with people. Cain knew he never would have gotten this date if Abel hadn't arranged it.

"Now, don't stay out too late, boys," Eve said, fussing with Abel's robe. "And act like gentlemen, the way we've raised you."

"We promise," Abel said, and gave Eve a quick peck on the cheek. "Let's get going, Cain."

Amber and Tiffany's tent wasn't that far from Cain and Abel's. The girls were already waiting for them in their front field.

"It's such a nice night, we decided to wait outside," Tiffany said. She walked over to Abel and draped her arm around his.

Amber moved next to Cain, but made no such affectionate gesture. Cain was relieved. He wouldn't have known how to move if Amber were attached to him.

"Shall we go for a walk?" Abel asked. "The night is young and the moon is full."

Amber and Tiffany giggled. Abel frequently made Eve giggle, so Cain knew it was a good sound.

"Tiffany, you look especially lovely tonight," Abel said as he and Tiffany led the way.

Tiffany giggled some more.

"You look good, too, Amber," Cain said. "Even nicer than Tiffany."

"Oh, Cain," Amber said, but she and Tiffany giggled, so Cain supposed he hadn't made too big a mistake.

Abel led them to an empty field near the now deserted Garden of Eden. The two couples sat down under a tree.

"Oh, it's an apple tree," Tiffany said. "You know, the other day, my mother brought yours an apple pie, and your mother just went crazy. She practically threw the pie at Mom."

"She's allergic to apples," Abel said smoothly. "Can't even bear the smell of them."

"I've never heard her say a good thing about serpents either," Cain said.

Amber shuddered. "I hate serpents," she said. "You'll protect me from them, won't you, Cain?"

"All right," Cain said. He almost wished for a serpent to arrive, just so he could batter it to death.

"Now that we're here, what should we do?" Tiffany asked.

"I can think of a few things," Abel said, and the girls giggled some more.

Cain was used to not getting the joke, but he started to wish Abel and Tiffany weren't around. He'd be much more likely to find a serpent to kill if they weren't making so much noise.

"I have an idea," Abel said. "It came to me this afternoon, while I was sowing in the field. It's called dancing. Come on, Tiffany. I think you'll really like it."

"What's dancing?" she asked as Abel pulled her up off the ground.

"It's when you move your body to music," Abel replied. "I invented music today, too." He pursed his lips together and made a funny bird-like sound. "I call that whistling," he said. "But there's singing, too. La la la la la."

"Oh, I like that," Amber said. "Now show us dancing, Abel."

Abel raised his hands over his head and bent them until his fingertips touched. Then he hopped from one foot to the other, landing on his soles.

The girls laughed and applauded. Cain personally thought Abel looked pretty dumb.

"That's just one way to dance," Abel said. "Here's another." He lowered his arms and began swinging them around, while kicking first his left leg and then his right. He sang, "La la la la la," until Tiffany and Amber joined in. Soon they were kicking their legs and hopping around.

"Try it, Cain," Amber said. "Dancing is fun."

Cain lumbered up and tried to jerk his body around the way his brother did. But he felt like a fool, and he knew he looked like one as well. "I'm no good at this," he said.

"Then make music," Abel said. "Go 'la la la' while the three of us dance."

So Cain stood there endlessly singing, "La la la la la," while Abel and the two dates kicked and hopped and swung one another around. They were clearly having a great time, and Cain wished he knew how to dance along with them. Maybe he'd practice sometime in the field. Cain was pretty sure the animals wouldn't laugh at his efforts.

"That was great," Tiffany said. "But Amber and I need to freshen up in the ladies' room. If you'll excuse us."

"Certainly," Abel said.

Cain didn't know what a ladies' room was. He wasn't even sure what a "ladies" was. But before he had a chance to ask, the girls began walking to a nearby bush. Cain could hear them whispering and giggling as they walked.

"That Abel is so cute."

"He certainly is."

Cain could feel the rage rising within him as it so often did. Things came so easily for Abel. He already had Tiffany. What did he need Amber for?

"Girls," Abel said, sounding as though he'd spent his whole life surrounded by them. "That Amber is real sweet for you. I can tell."

"You think so?" Cain asked.

Abel nodded. "But you have to do something," he said. "Girls go for guys who know how to do things."

Cain racked his brains to think what he knew the others didn't. By the time Amber and Tiffany returned from the bush, Cain had figured out what he could show them.

"Follow me," he said, and he was gratified when the others did. "See this?" he said, pointing to a tree branch.

"What's that hanging off the branch?" Amber asked.

"It's a basket," Cain said. "I found it. Abel must have left it out in the field during a rainstorm, because its bottom is rotted out."

"Abel wouldn't do that," Tiffany said.

Abel grinned. "Sometimes I get a little careless," he admitted. The way he said it, though, being careless was somehow admirable.

"Anyway, I tied the basket to the branch," Cain said. "And see that coconut? I throw it up in the air and see if I can get it to go through the basket. I call it basketcoconut."

"Why would you do that?" Tiffany asked.

Cain couldn't think of an answer. All he knew was it was the only thing he had ever invented and it meant a lot to him.

"I think that could be a lot of fun," Abel said. "And I bet it's harder than it looks. You know what? We could invent something called a game. That's when everyone has a chance and whoever does best wins."

"Wins what?" Tiffany asked.

"Say the first person to get the coconut into the basket gets to kiss whoever they want," Abel suggested. "How does that sound, girls?"

Tiffany and Amber giggled their approval.

"Cain should go first," Abel said. "Since he invented basket-coconut. Come on, Cain. Show us how it works."

Cain picked up the coconut and tossed it toward the basket. It missed by half a foot.

"Tiffany, you go next," Abel said.

"Ooh, the coconut is heavy," Tiffany said. "Abel, help me toss it in."

"My pleasure," Abel said. He put his arms around Tiffany's, and the two of them tossed the coconut together. It landed nowhere near the basket.

"Amber?" Abel asked as he retrieved the coconut.

Amber shook her head. "You go," she said. "I'll wait for last."

Abel tried throwing the coconut underhanded. It came closer to the basket, but didn't go in.

"My turn," Amber said. She picked up the coconut and took up a spot about six feet from the basket. Then she held the coconut with her two hands at chest level, sprang up, and threw it straight into the basket.

"You did it!" Tiffany squealed. "You won the gome!"

"Game," Abel said. "You certainly did, Amber. Now you get to kiss whoever you want."

Cain waited in dread. Sure enough, Amber took a couple of steps toward Abel. Then she stopped, looked at Tiffany, and giggled. She turned around, trotted toward Cain, and kissed him right on the lips.

Cain turned bright red with pleasure. She did like him after all. And he hadn't even had to kill a serpent.

"Well, girls, I think it's time we took you home," Abel said. For a moment, Cain thought Abel sounded jealous, but then he laughed at himself for even thinking such a ridiculous thought.

"You two go ahead," Amber said. "Cain and I will catch up with you later."

"Are you sure?" Abel asked.

"We're sure," Amber replied.

Tiffany grabbed Abel's arm, but Abel shook her off. "See you later, Cain," he said.

"I thought they'd never leave," Amber said. "Let's go back to the field, Cain. I have an idea."

Cain had an idea of his own. He took Amber's hand and held it as they walked together. Amber's fingers entwined his and Cain was enthralled with how small and delicate they were.

"Dancing was fun," Amber said as they stood in the moonlight.

"But it would be a lot more fun if we did it holding each other."

"Like this?" Cain asked. He put his hands on Amber's back, and was gratified when she draped her arms over his shoulders. They held each other so close Cain couldn't be sure where his breathing stopped and Amber's began.

"La la la la la," Amber sang softly as she and Cain swayed rhythmically together. Amber was right, Cain thought. Dancing was a lot better when you did it together.

Soon Amber had stopped singing, but she and Cain continued to move to the music in their heads. "You're beautiful," Cain whispered. "I never knew anyone could be as beautiful as you."

"Oh, Cain," Amber sighed. "You know just the right thing to say."

"Amber! Amber, get on home right now!"

Amber broke away from Cain's embrace. "That's Mom," she said. "I'd better get back."

"I'll walk with you," Cain said. He took Amber's hand and held it tenderly as they made their way to her tent.

"You don't have to come in with me," Amber said. "I'll say good night to you here." She stood still and smiled. "I kissed you, Cain. Aren't you going to kiss me?"

Cain bent down and kissed her. His heart was giddy with happiness he could never have imagined.

"Good night, my darling Cain," Amber said. "This was the best date any girl has ever had." With that, she sprinted toward her tent.

Cain watched as first her shadow and then Amber herself arrived at the tent. When he was sure she was all right, he turned around and began dancing in the moonlight toward home.

Even from a distance, he could hear his parents squabbling. It didn't matter what the words were. The fights all had to do with something Eve had done that Adam had never forgiven her for.

Cain paused for a moment, not wanting the perfection of the moment to be spoiled by his parents' anger. But then he heard them laughing. *Abel must be home*, he thought. Only Abel could make them laugh that way.

That Abel was quite some fellow, Cain told himself as he stopped gliding and began walking. Coming up with dates and music and dancing and games all in one day. He was bound to be a success, no matter what he chose to do.

Cain pictured himself all grown. He'd be married, maybe even to Amber, and he'd have lots of kids. He and his wife would work together and love each other and they would never fight. It would be a good life, Cain was sure of it. He'd work long and hard if he had to, but somehow, someday, he knew he'd make his mark.

Interview ⟳ SUSAN BETH PFEFFER

"Cain and Abel Double-Date" is a wonderfully outrageous concept. How did you happen to come up with it for a story on growing up Jewish?

I went through a lot of different story ideas. But I wasn't satisfied with any of them. A couple of days before Passover, I went to the Cooper-Hewitt Museum with a friend of mine. She takes a long time at museums, and I run through them. The Cooper-Hewitt turned out to be a very small museum, and after examining its exhibits and checking out the gift shop item by item, I had a lot of time to kill.

I found a chair in the basement (it's not a sitter friendly museum) and willed myself to come up with a story idea. First I went through all the holidays, but nothing struck me. Then I started thinking about the Bible. I played with the idea of a story about a handmaiden of Vashti's, and her sudden switch of bosses, but I wasn't crazy about it.

Then I thought, Cain and Abel double-date.

I loved the idea. I wasn't at all sure I could pull it off, wasn't even sure it was acceptable, since Cain and Abel aren't exactly Jewish. But it didn't matter. Sometimes you get an idea, and sometimes an idea gets you. I knew I had to write this story.

So the next day, instead of helping my eighty-six-year-old mother prepare for the Seder, I stayed home and wrote "Cain and Abel Double-Date." I have a very understanding mother. The Seder got off to a late start, but that's also a tradition in our family.

So you grew up in a traditional Jewish family?

I grew up very Jewish. My father's father was a rabbi, a Talmudic scholar of great reputation. (Although he died ten years before I was born, I have met people who've asked if I'm related to him.) My father, Leo Pfeffer, was special counsel for the American Jewish Congress. My brother and I attended a Jewish day school for most of our elementary education. We studied Hebrew daily, celebrated the holidays, went to synagogue every Saturday, and rooted for any and all Jewish athletes.

There aren't too many laughs in Genesis, but your story is funny.
Was irreverent humor a part of your family tradition?

My father was a very funny man, and he liked the fact that I was funny as well. His father's dying words had been a pun, and my father took great pride in that fact. Humor was an integral part of our household. My father said when he was a young man he stumbled onto an early Marx Brothers movie and was stunned to hear his kind of humor coming from the screen.

If you were Jewish, you were supposed to be funny. Our Seders weren't sedate, boring events. They were filled with songs (some made up for the occasion), jokes, questions (far more than the traditional four), and intellectual arguments. Our Sabbath dinners were like that as well, only they didn't take as long and you got to eat challah.

Tradition, in other words, doesn't rule out individuality?

One of the things I like best about Judaism is it offers you a lot of options. You don't have to believe exactly the same as other Jews believe; you don't have to obey exactly the same as other Jews obey; you don't have to observe exactly the same as other Jews observe. There are core values and core beliefs and core traditions, but there's a lot of room to maneuver. All the Jews may be at Seders the first night of Passover, but that doesn't mean all the Seders have to be the same.

And between the Torah and the Marx Brothers, there's a lot to enjoy about being a Jew.

Biography ⁓ SUSAN BETH PFEFFER

Susan Beth Pfeffer is the author of more than sixty books for children and young adults. Among her titles are *About David* (winner of the South Carolina Young Adult Book Award), *Kid Power* (winner of the Dorothy Canfield Fisher and Sequoyah Children's Book Awards), and *The Year Without Michael* (named one of the one hundred best books written for teenagers between 1968 and 1993 by the American Library Association). Ms. Pfeffer has also written *Turning Thirteen*, an untraditional Bat Mitzvah story, and *Twice Taken*. She is the author of the popular *Portraits of Little Women* series as well. She lives in the town of Wallkill, New York.

Pinch-Hitting

by Phyllis Shalant

The last place my grandma Hannah went as a free agent was to my Bat Mitzvah. Dressed in her peach chiffon party dress with shoes dyed to match, she looked stylish and even pretty, in a grandmalike way. My mother had been very worried about her memory, but Grandma Hannah knew the faces and the names of relatives I'd only vaguely remembered hearing about. And when I introduced her to my temple classmates, she said things like, "Rachel's told me a lot about you." She seemed fine to me.

When it was time for the service to begin I took my place between the rabbi and the cantor at the *bimah*, which is the platform where we unroll and read the sacred scrolls. I was nervous, but when I looked out over the congregation I saw Grandma Hannah, her face full of pride, looking right back at me. It was just how she looked at every event of mine she'd ever attended—school plays, piano recitals, softball games. No matter whether I flubbed lines or notes, or dropped the ball, she held me in her eyes as if I were wonderful. She even called the wrinkles around her eyes "happiness creases" because she said they came from smiling at me so much. And in spite of my nerves I saw those familiar, comforting little lines, and I felt a sense of calm taking over.

During a Bar or Bat Mitzvah at our temple, your parents and grand-parents are called to the *bimah* so the Torah scroll can be passed from the eldest to the youngest. The custom symbolizes how the covenant between God and the Jews is passed from generation to generation. When it was time, the rabbi called up my parents, Grandma Hannah, and also my father's parents, Grandma Ethel and Grandpa Fred, who were visiting us from halfway across the country. We stood side by side in a little line facing the congregation, and the rabbi placed the Torah in the arms of Grandpa Fred, who was at the far end. I was mostly worried that Grandma Ethel, who is awfully frail and can only see out of one eye, would drop the scroll when Grandpa passed it to her. But she held the Torah like a champion weight lifter and passed it on to Grandma Hannah—who pushed it away so hard, my father had to catch both Grandma Ethel and the Torah.

"I can't watch the baby anymore, Mama!" Grandma Hannah shouted. "I have to go to school."

"Grandma!" I gasped.

"It's all right, Rachel," my mother whispered. She placed a hand on my shoulder for an instant before she walked over to Grandma Han-nah and said calmly, "Come with me, Hannah."

"I've missed too much school already," Grandma Hannah told her.

"I know. I'll help you get ready," my mother replied. "Come." She held out her hand.

Grandma Hannah took it and allowed herself to be led down from the *bimah* and out of the room.

For a few seconds there was absolute silence among the members of the congregation. Then the whispering started. I must've been frozen until the rabbi sidled over to my dad and me. "I'm sorry this had to happen now—or at all," he murmured. "We could take a few mo-ments for a musical interlude. It would give us a chance to see if Claire and Hannah will be able to come back."

"That sounds like a good idea," my father answered. "I'll go see where they went."

"I'll go, too," I added. My father opened his mouth as if to disagree.

But then he looked in my eyes and nodded. He took my hand and we stepped off the *bimah* as the cantor began playing her guitar and singing "Go Out in Joy."

We found Mom and Grandma Hannah sitting on folding chairs in the coatroom. "Rachel, I'm sorry I ruined your Bat Mitzvah," my grandmother said, as soon as she saw us.

"No, you didn't, Grandma. I still have to read my Torah portion. Are you coming back inside?" I asked.

She picked a loose thread from her sleeve and rolled it back and forth between her thumb and forefinger. "Everyone will stare at me."

"No, they won't," my mother said. "They'll understand. We all say the wrong thing sometimes, Ma."

"That's right," my father added. "Wait till you hear me try to say the Torah blessing."

"Please, Grandma. I want you to be there." I wanted to touch my grandmother, but I was afraid. It was so weird because I'd always hugged her before.

"Okay, I'll come." My grandmother nodded as if she were very tired. She looked at my mother from out of the corner of her eye. "Will my mama still be there?" she asked.

The doctors weren't sure what was wrong with her. Some thought Alzheimer's, others a series of ministrokes, and some suggested hardening of the arteries. But they all agreed she wasn't likely to get better, and would probably get worse. Which she did right away. For the eighteen years since her husband, my grandpa Abe, died, Grandma Hannah had lived by herself in a cozy apartment in the city. She was an expert at growing miniature fruit trees indoors and when you stepped into the apartment, you immediately smelled this fresh, citrusy scent from her tiny lemons, limes, and oranges. Her walls were full of family photographs. She even had framed pictures of my animals, which she called her "grand-pets" (a hermit crab and a black cat named Felix).

But now her life no longer seemed safe. My mother got a call from a policeman who picked up Grandma Hannah while she was waiting at a bus stop. She told him she was on her way to her Wednesday afternoon canasta game at her friend Mrs. Shapiro's. Except it was Friday at three o'clock in the morning when the policeman found her. And only a few days later, she put the kettle on for tea and forgot about it. What's weird is the thing whistled and whistled and she didn't get it—that it was her own kettle whistling, I mean. We were all lucky that a neighbor in the apartment next door heard it before the water boiled completely away. Otherwise, there might have been a fire.

It was obvious that Grandma Hannah needed to be supervised twenty-four hours a day, so my mother began investigating nursing homes. I couldn't stop thinking how Grandma Hannah used to resist when Mom and Dad would suggest she move closer to us. "I don't know if my lungs could get used to air without pollution," she'd always begin. Then she'd say more seriously, "Here in the city, if I run out of milk, I can walk down the street and buy a quart. I can take a bus to the library or the beauty parlor or the doctor. Out there, I'd have to depend on you to drive me everywhere. You'd be sick of me in no time."

But no one was giving my grandmother a choice anymore. My parents simply announced that she had to move. I almost hated them that day. But even worse than that, I hated that Grandma Hannah didn't refuse. I could hardly stand to look in her eyes because of the way fear had made her pupils like a doll's—glassy and impenetrable.

On the days Mom went to inspect nursing homes, she'd come home and lock herself in her room for hours. I always offered to go with her the next time, but she'd say, "It's better if you don't come, Rachel. I want you to feel like a normal eighth grader for as long as possible."

Only I wasn't normal. I felt as if my insides had become an eerie, frozen landscape—a cave with my heart and lungs and other organs turned into stalactites and stalagmites. When my friends called, I got off the phone quickly. I couldn't think of anything to say and I was no longer interested in the latest gossip. I hardly looked at my pets, except to do the basics like feeding and cleaning, although a few times, I even forgot to feed Felix. And I refused to go to the Tuesday afternoon confirmation class at our synagogue, or even the youth group meetings on Sundays.

"Rachel, it would be good for you to go to temple," my mother said. "Your friends are there. You could talk to Rabbi Marcus about what you're feeling. Or you could just talk to God."

"God? God let this happen to Grandma Hannah at my Bat Mitzvah!" I snapped. "I am never talking to God again!"

In September of my freshman year in high school—exactly four months after my Bat Mitzvah—we moved Grandma Hannah into Honeywood Farms. The place had nothing to do with farming—no crops or animals or even a barn—but I guess no one wants to move into a place called a nursing home.

From the outside, Honeywood Farms actually resembled the apartment house where Grandma Hannah had lived in the city, a six-story brick building with a small evergreen tree in a planter on either side of the front door. The lobby wasn't bad either—sofas in that mauve color that grandmothers seem to favor, end tables with stacks of magazines like Good Housekeeping, and a cageful of parakeets that twittered cheerfully.

Grandma Hannah's room was on the sixth floor. She had a "private," although some residents shared. On the day she moved in, I carried her mini-lime tree in one arm and the mini-lemon tree in the other. Dad had the mini-orange. "This is sure a nice, big window, Grandma," I said as we set them on the sill.

She came over and ran a finger across a glossy leaf. "It's a north window, Rachel. Nothing grows in a north window."

"I'll bring a grow light the next time I come," my mother said. "Your plants won't know the difference."

Grandma Hannah just sat on the edge of the bed without answering. Meanwhile, my father hung family photos all over the walls, and my mother put Grandma's clothes away.

"I'll visit you after school as often as I can," I promised. "One of our school bus routes goes right by here and I can probably arrange to get dropped off. I'll take the public bus back home."

My grandmother was smoothing the mauve bedspread over and over with the flat of her hand. She nodded without looking up.

It seemed like only a short time had gone by before a voice said, "Time for dinner, Mrs. Birnbaum." We all looked toward the doorway where a huge woman in a blue uniform hovered.

"I . . . I'm not hungry," my grandmother whispered.

"It don't matter. We got to get you on the schedule," the woman said. She had a little badge pinned above her bosom that read SALLY DEAN, NURSE AIDE. "Come with me. I'll show you where the dining room is." The badge rose and fell like a tiny ship on a stormy sea when she spoke.

I looked at my watch. "But it's only a quarter to five."

"Our people eat early," the aide said. "They got to digest their food so they can go to bed at nine."

Nine? Grandma Hannah liked to stay up and watch the *Tonight Show* at eleven thirty. I looked at my mother. She wouldn't meet my eyes. My father began fumbling in his toolbox.

Grandma Hannah brushed a strand of hair from her cheek. "I'll need a few minutes to get ready."

"I don't got time to wait. Besides, this ain't a beauty pageant."

"I'll help my grandmother find the dining room. You can go," I said.

"Rachel!" my mother whispered. "Don't be rude!"

Sally Dean shrugged. "Don't bother me one bit. Lots of people come in here high and mighty, but none of 'em stay that way." When she squinted at my grandma, her pale white cheeks puffed up like two lumps of rising challah dough. I felt like punching them back down.

"Just give us a few minutes," my mother pleaded quietly.

"Suit yourself. But if she misses this meal, she's going to be mighty uncomfortable later. We don't got room service here."

"I'm going to report her!" I squealed as Sally Dean's big blue butt lumbered off down the corridor.

"She was unnecessarily abrupt . . ." My mother's voice trailed off as if she were considering.

"Don't cause trouble." Grandma Hannah stood up. "I'll wash up and go downstairs to dinner with Rachel. I'll pick a little."

✳

I quickly settled into a routine of visiting Grandma Hannah on Tuesday and Friday afternoons. Tuesday was an especially good choice because it was the day the confirmation class met at temple. My father took going to temple seriously—he was on the synagogue's board of directors—and he was always trying to persuade me to continue my religious education. But once Tuesday became one of my "Grandma Hannah Days," he stopped trying to pressure me into going.

Fridays were good because, from 3:30 P.M. to 4:30 P.M., Matthew Pepper came and played his guitar for the residents of Honeywood Farms. Matt was friendly, cheerful, and fun to be around. He'd started playing at Honeywood while his grandmother was a resident there and just kept on coming after she died. Even though he was only a year older than I, he seemed really comfortable around the residents of Honeywood. It made me want to be like him.

Each week after Matt played his last song, the residents had a brief cheese-and-crackers social. Matt and I would spend a few minutes talking and laughing. We both thought it was really funny how the residents called his music "rock and roll," even though he played stuff like "If I Had a Hammer" and "Puff the Magic Dragon."

Afterward, Grandma Hannah and I always went back to her room and played cards until dinner. Although my grandma used to be a killer canasta player, we played games with simple rules like war or go fish. One afternoon, we began playing war. I turned over a six of clubs and Grandma Hannah turned over a three of hearts. I reached out to take the two cards, but my grandma scooped them up first. "My card beats yours," she said.

I stared at the cards. "The six was mine, Grandma."

"I know." There was a little edge to her voice that gave me goose bumps. My grandmother never used that tone with me. "Next card, Rachel," she demanded.

I turned over the top card on my pile. It was a nine of spades. Grandma Hannah flipped over a four of diamonds.

She turned her head and gave me this funny sideways glance. "I win, right?"

I felt like a company of fire trucks was racing across my chest, alarms screeching, but I forced myself to smile. "High card always wins, Grandma." I reached for the cards. So did she.

"Grandma . . ." I fought to keep my voice from rising.

She snatched up the cards and clutched them to her chest. "These are mine."

Suddenly I was shouting. "Act your age, Grandma! Stop pretending you don't know how to play! This is just a stupid game!" I threw my cards down on the table.

Grandma Hannah just looked at me. Her expression wasn't angry or even hurt. She seemed confused, as if she wasn't sure what had just happened.

"Dinnertime, Hannah."

I didn't have to look up. I knew it was Sally Dean. Usually, I managed to avoid her. If I passed her in the hall, I looked the other way. If she was waiting for the elevator when I was leaving, I lingered at the water fountain, and took the next one down. If she was in my grandma's room changing the linens or watering the mini-citrus trees—which she seemed to like better than people—I walked down the corridor pretending to be interested in the paintings on the wall until she left.

But now my face was scalding as I wondered if she'd heard me yell at my grandmother. "It's okay, I'll clean up the cards. You go to dinner, Grandma," I murmured.

Grandma Hannah looked toward the closet. "I want my sweater."

"I sent it down to be washed this morning. It ain't back yet. It's too hot in the dining room, anyways." Sally Dean was always sweating. Dark stains often showed near the armpits of her blue uniform.

Like a small child, Grandma Hannah crossed her arms over her chest and held her shoulders as if she were cold.

I jumped up from the bed. "You can wear your blue blazer to dinner, Grandma," I said, flinging open her closet door.

"My sweater," Grandma Hannah repeated blankly.

"I just told you it ain't back. You think they're waiting down there to wash your things one at a time?"

"Don't talk to her like that!" I shouted. But it was my own cruel words that were still echoing inside my head.

"You think you're doing her a favor coddling her, but you're just making things harder. You know there ain't no reasoning with her. She's just got to learn to accept things." Sally Dean plodded over to my grandmother and held out her hand. "Now come on, Hannah."

Grandma Hannah took her hand and stood up. I didn't kiss her good-bye.

I was standing at the bus stop shaking and sniffling into my coat sleeve when Matt Pepper drove up. "You look like you need a ride, Rachel. Get in."

So with my nose running and the ends of my hair wet with tears, I yanked open the door. Another time I might have laughed about it— or run away shrieking.

"What's wrong?" Matt asked.

"Everything! My grandma can't even play a simple card game anymore. I got so upset, I screamed at her." I was glad Matt had to keep his eyes on the road so he couldn't see mine welling up again.

"I know how you feel," Matt said. "The first time my grandmother forgot what floor she lived on I was so frustrated I yelled at her, too." Matt surprised me by cracking a smile. "The good thing was, when I apologized later, she had no idea what I was talking about. She'd forget the bad stuff as well as the good."

That only made me cry harder. "That bitch, Sally Dean, treats my grandma like she's a prisoner. I hate her."

Matt cleared his throat. "You know, the staff works really hard, especially the nurses aides. You can see how easy it is for them to get burned out, spending day after day in that place."

"It's their job! They're getting paid to do it. If they don't like it they should quit!"

"And who would take care of the residents?" Matt asked softly.

"I don't want to talk about it anymore." I shifted closer to the window and looked out.

"Fine." Matt turned on the radio and we didn't talk about anything at all.

At home after dinner, I stretched out on my bed with a scruffy copy of *The True Confessions of Charlotte Doyle*. I first read it two years ago and I was probably too old for it now. But I liked to reread it whenever I was feeling down—which lately was more and more often. A knock on my open door made me look up.

"Got a minute?" my father asked.

I forced a little smile. "Oh, I dunno, I'm kinda bee-zee."

Dad stepped in and sat on my desk chair. "I thought you'd like to know that the temple board voted to do our Pinch Hitter's program at Honeywood Farms this year."

The Pinch Hitter's program! I'd forgotten all about it. Each year on Christmas Day, the members of our congregation perform a mitzvah—the Hebrew word for a good deed—by filling in for the nonprofessional staff at a local hospital or nursing home. That way, we give the workers who celebrate Christmas a chance to stay home with their families. Adults and teenagers are both eligible to participate, so our temple brings out quite a crew. Last year, I distributed food trays at our community hospital.

"So, Rachel, you'll sign up with the youth group?"

I had to hand it to my dad. He'd been yearning for me to come back to temple—and Christmas at Honeywood with the youth group was a first step. He knew I couldn't refuse. Still I said, "Could I at least think about it?"

"Sure, honeybee." He patted my knee and walked out whistling.

By the week before Christmas our temple had enough pinch hitters signed up to assist the Honeywood residents on a one-to-one basis. Of course I was assigned to Grandma Hannah. I was to arrive on Christmas morning at nine o'clock and stay until Grandma's dinner at five.

"Spending the day with my own grandmother doesn't seem like

much of a contribution to society," I told my parents the night before. "I go to Honeywood twice a week anyway."

"Not for eight hours at a stretch," my mother answered. "Wait until the day is over. Then see if you don't feel like you've performed a mitzvah."

I rode over to Honeywood in a minivan with some of my temple classmates—or former classmates. I'd been nervous about seeing them after being absent all fall, but they were excited about the day ahead and everyone asked me questions about what the Honeywood residents were like. There was even a group of kids that had been practicing holiday songs so they could entertain the residents. It was easy to relax and get into the spirit.

"Surprise, Grandma!" I said as I walked into her room. "I'm going to spend the whole day with you."

She was eating toast and jelly and there was a sticky spot of purple on her chin. Her eyes darted around the room before she spoke. "Where's Sally?"

"It's Christmas today. I guess she's home with her family." I picked up a napkin and dabbed at the jelly spot. "Aren't you glad to see me?"

"Yes, darling." She looked away. "Sally helps me get dressed."

"I'll help you, Grandma. Quit worrying! We're going to have fun today."

While she was in the bathroom, I made the bed. Then I searched through her drawers and picked out a soft red sweater I hadn't seen her wear in a while. Usually when I came, my grandmother was wearing the same old navy cardigan.

"I don't want to wear that," she said.

"It's festive. Red's a real Christmas color."

"It's not mine."

"Sure it is. You used to wear it all the time."

My grandmother twisted her pajama top in her hands. "I . . . I want to save it."

I thought her voice sounded about as high as it could get before it broke into crying. I tried to keep mine light and steady. "Okay,

Grandma." I opened her drawer. "You pick something out."

"This." She pulled out the old navy sweater.

"Great."

My grandmother smiled at me.

I helped her get into her things, which sounds easier than it was, especially putting her socks on. I combed her hair, buttoned her sweater, and put toothpaste on her toothbrush. Finally, we were finished.

"Okay, what do you want to do today?" I asked.

"I'm hungry," Grandma Hannah said.

I looked at my watch. "Lunch isn't for another two hours."

"Sally knows how to get snacks."

I remembered that there was a vending machine on the ground floor. "So do I. Let's go for a ride in the elevator," I suggested.

As we passed by the lobby, Matt was coming in the front door. I felt my face start flushing like those blinking Christmas lights. "Hi," I said. "I didn't know you were coming today."

"I didn't know you were coming either," he said teasingly. He turned to my grandmother. "Hi, Hannah, how are you?"

"Fine. How else could I be with Nurse Rachel to take care of me?" She patted my arm.

Every once in a while Grandma Hannah could act like her old self—warm, funny, and kind. I wanted the moment to last forever.

"Want to have lunch together?" Matt asked.

"I'm eating with my grandma. They're serving lunch in the residents' rooms today because of the holiday."

"Okay if I bring a tray in and join you two?"

"That'd be great," I said. Then Grandma Hannah tugged at my sleeve. "I want my snack now."

The vending machine was outside the staff lounge. It didn't have a very healthy selection, just packages of cream-filled cupcakes, potato chips, chocolate bars, cheese crackers, pretzels, and gum.

While I fished for change in my pocket I wondered if this was where Sally got my grandmother her snacks. And if so, who paid for them? "Do you want cheese crackers or pretzels, Grandma?" I asked.

"I want a chocolate bar."

When I was little and my grandmother used to baby-sit for me, she'd prepare healthy snacks like Cheerios and raisins, or peanut butter on apple slices. "It's too early for chocolate, Grandma. How about the crackers?"

"Sally lets me have chocolate," my grandma said. She actually began tugging at the plunger under the chocolate bar.

Sally doesn't care if your insides rot! I wanted to tell her. But I only said, "Okay, Gram, whatever you want." I put my quarters in and held my breath. If the machine was out of chocolate bars, I was afraid of what Grandma Hannah might do. Beat the machine to a pulp, maybe. Or cry.

Two women volunteers were running a project in the arts and crafts room—wall hangings made with dried flowers and paper plates. We sat down at a table to put one together. But every time her fingers got a spot of Magic Marker or glue on them, Grandma Hannah had to wash them in the sink. She was up and down like a jack-in-the-box. Finally, I finished the project for her while she watched. "You did a very good job," she complimented me.

"We can hang it up in your room," I said.

A worried look came over her face. "No, you take it home." She pushed it toward me as if it were diseased.

Once there was a time when her house was filled with my crayon drawings and ceramic candy dishes. "I'll keep it, Grandma," I said. "It'll look good over my bed."

When we got back to her room, our lunch trays had already been dropped off. I uncovered our dishes. "Look, Grandma, chicken soup, turkey, mashed potatoes, and peas and carrots. And ice cream with chocolate syrup for dessert."

Matt appeared at the door, carrying his tray. "Is this Hannah's Cafe?"

But Grandma Hannah didn't answer. She was already tucking into her lunch—ice cream first. I remembered a bumper sticker I'd seen around: "Life is uncertain. Eat dessert first." I used to think of it as a joke.

Matt sat on a chair and balanced his tray on his lap. We tried to chat, but both of us kept watching Grandma Hannah. She put a spoonful of ice cream in her coffee and tasted it. That didn't seem like a bad idea. But then she took another spoonful of ice cream and dropped it in her chicken soup. She ate it without wincing. Then she began putting ice cream on her turkey and peas and carrots.

"Grandma, I don't think that'll taste very good," I said.

"No?" she said, without stopping what she was doing.

I reached for her hand, but she jerked it away.

"Maybe we should try ours that way," Matt said. "It might be delicious." I knew he was trying to make me feel better, but I only burst into tears. Grandma Hannah didn't even seem to notice.

"Rachel, I didn't mean to . . ."

"I know. It's just that I hate how things are." I blew my nose into my napkin. "Could you go?" I sniffled.

"Sure." Matt stood up. "Rachel? Hannah must have been a really terrific person. I can tell by how you feel about her now." He gave my shoulder a gentle pat.

After lunch, Grandma Hannah seemed tired. It wasn't hard to get her to lie down on her bed for a rest. "I want to look at the pictures," she said, pointing to the album of photos from my Bat Mitzvah that she kept on her night table.

I hadn't opened my own Bat Mitzvah album once after Grandma Hannah moved to Honeywood. I was afraid my grandmother would find it as sad as I did.

"Maybe we should look at something else."

"No, the pictures."

I sat next to her and began turning pages.

"My peach dress," she said. "So pretty."

"You look beautiful there, Grandma," I told her.

On the next page were pictures of me reading from the Torah. "You gave me such *nachas* up there, Rachel," Grandma Hannah said, using the Yiddish expression for making someone proud.

I turned the page to a group of photos that had been taken at the reception after the ceremony. "Look, there's Aunt Sophie on the dance floor."

"She can shake her tush like she's standing on an earthquake," my grandmother commented. We both started laughing.

From outside the room, there was a cough. I looked up and saw Sally Dean gazing at us. She was wearing her coat and carrying a potted plant tied with a red ribbon.

I must've gaped at her before I managed to say, "Merry Christmas, Sally."

"I forgot to give this to Hannah yesterday. It's a carrot fern. I grow 'em by sprouting carrot tops."

"It's pretty, isn't it, Grandma?" I said.

Sally set it on the windowsill next to the fruit trees. She didn't take off her coat and she didn't walk out. "Hannah and I always look at those photos together," she said. "Makes her happier than anything else."

"Really?" I whispered.

"I've always wondered who some of those people are. Hannah doesn't remember all of 'em anymore."

I swallowed. "Want me to tell you?"

Sally pulled up a chair.

At first we didn't notice that Grandma Hannah had fallen asleep. Not until she began snoring, anyway. Sally smiled at her and stood up.

"You seem to have managed very well today, miss."

I shook my head. "All she ate was a chocolate bar and some ice cream. And I'm exhausted."

I thought she was going to say, "I told you so." Or something about my spoiling Grandma Hannah. Instead she just shrugged. "Well, some days is better than others."

"Thank you, Sally," I said as she was leaving.

She turned and gave me a short nod. "You're welcome."

While Grandma Hannah slept, I looked through the rest of the photos. I was thinking about how much had happened since that day. I felt like a different person now. I thought I might even go back to religious school in the spring.

When my grandmother awoke, I would be there for her, just as she had always been there for me. It was like the covenant we'd sealed at my Bat Mitzvah; a sacred responsibility passed from one generation to the next. And one I planned to honor for as long as I could.

Interview ⤳ PHYLLIS SHALANT

What inspired you to write "Pinch-Hitting"?
My mother had Alzheimer's disease. She spent her last three years in a nursing home, and it was a difficult adjustment for everyone in our family. Although we didn't yet know what they meant, we started seeing signs of the disease around the time of the Bat Mitzvah of my younger daughter, Jenny. My mother was actually a half hour late to Jenny's service because she got lost on the way to the temple.

It's easy to displace the anger you feel toward a disease by directing it at institutions and caregivers. But the truth is, dementia is a frustrating, sometimes frightening, condition that's hard on everyone.

Tell us about your own experience of growing up Jewish.
In a way, my experience was a schizophrenic one. We lived in an area of Brooklyn, New York, where, in the 1950s, many Jews lived. As a result, when I was a very young child, the whole world seemed Jewish to me. I didn't attend religious school; it was mostly boys who had Bar Mitzvahs in those days, although a few girls I knew had them, too. My parents didn't even belong to a temple, although they always went to say *yizkor* on Yom Kippur. But I was surrounded by Jewish families and my identity as a Jew was pretty secure.

But all that time, another message was getting through to me. The two Catholic girls who lived in the apartment next door to mine regularly told me that "Jews killed Christ." The mother of my non-Jewish best friend often slipped me pamphlets urging me to accept Christ or "burn in eternity." When I was eleven or twelve years old, I read *The Diary of Anne Frank*. After that, every night before I fell asleep I would think up ways of hiding or escaping in case the Nazis came back.

So, even in a "Jewish neighborhood," you felt different?
Even those of us living among many Jews sometimes feel like outsiders. We don't celebrate Christmas. Most of us don't look like the models in the J. Crew catalog. The reality of the Holocaust is always with us. In

some ways we're different at a time in our lives when everyone just wants to fit in. I wish kids could feel that different is okay.

Has your daughters' experience differed from yours?
After our daughters were born, my husband and I decided to join a temple. I wanted the girls to have a better understanding of what it meant to be Jewish than I'd had growing up. I especially valued the focus our religious school put on *tsedakah* (charity) and *tikkun olum* (making the world a better place). I based my novel *Shalom, Geneva Peace* on some of the experiences my older daughter, Emily, had in religious school, including serving Thanksgiving dinner at a soup kitchen in New York City.

After her Bat Mitzvah, Rachel moves away from formal temple activities but closer to adult responsibility and mitzvoth, genuine good deeds. Can you comment further about her actions in relation to her inner rebellion?
Part of growing up is accepting that not everything can be "made right" in the way our parents were able to solve our problems when we were little. Like a very young child, Rachel blames God for allowing Grandma Hannah's illness to happen. But her young adult self knows that illness strikes randomly. The strength people draw from their religious beliefs enables them to help themselves and one another. Rachel's kindness and commitment toward her grandmother are signs of her growing maturity, as is her step toward understanding and accepting Sally Dean. When Rachel decides to return to formal temple activities it will be as a young woman rather than as a child.

Biography ∽ PHYLLIS SHALANT

Phyllis Shalant's young adult novels include *Shalom, Geneva Peace;* *The Great Eye;* and *Beware of Kissing Lizard Lips,* which was listed in *School Library Journal's* "Sleepers: 100 Books Too Good to Miss." Her most recent novel, *Bartleby of the Mighty Mississippi,* is a fantasy for middle-grade readers. She is also the author of a series of activity books about world cultures: *Look What We've Brought You from Vietnam . . . Mexico . . . Korea . . . India . . .* and *the Caribbean.* Ms. Shalant lives in Westchester County, New York, where she also teaches writing classes to children and adults. "Pinch-Hitting" is dedicated to the memory of her mother, Anne Fischer Jushpy Scherwin.

The Rag Doll

by Ruth Minsky Sender

Lodz, Poland, 1936.

My name is Riva Minska. I am ten years old. I was born in Poland, as were my parents, my grandparents, my great-grandparents, and their ancestors.

Lodz is a big industrial city with many factories, schools, libraries, theaters, shops. The city is full of people, full of life. Men, women, and children fill the streets with the sounds of their voices, with the sounds of their footsteps. Some look happy, some look sad. Some walk fast, some stroll.

I often wonder. What is on their minds? What is waiting for them at their destination?

My destination is The Medem School, a small, private, Jewish day school. Classes are conducted in Yiddish and in Polish. In the public schools classes are held only in Polish.

"We have to work harder than the students in public schools," says Mrs. Melman, our Yiddish teacher. "Anti-Semitism . . ." She sighs painfully. "The Board of Education is looking for reasons to close the Jewish schools." She takes a deep breath. "We cannot let them win."

I look around me as I pass many streets on my long walk to school. Sometimes I see the signs of anti-Semitism on walls of buildings or store windows: DO NOT BUY FROM THE JEWS; JEWS, GO TO PALESTINE. I bite my lips.

Why? pounds in my head. *Jews have lived in Poland for a thousand years. We are part of Poland in every way. Why should I leave?*

"Ignore those ugly signs. Walk proudly." I hear Mama's soft voice.

School seems to be in turmoil this morning. Teachers, anxiety written on their faces, hurry students to their classrooms.

My first class is Polish. Our teacher, Miss Yoskowicz, moves a strand of hair away from her forehead. "Children." Her voice is low. "We will have a surprise visitor today, from the Board of Education." Her lips form a gentle smile. "Do not be alarmed. You are all bright students and lovely young people. Just be yourselves."

She begins her lesson on Polish literature. "Today we will read 'Pan Tadeush' by Adam Mickewicz. The poem is about freedom." She reads aloud: "Freedom, like good health is not valued while we have it. Only those who have lost freedom, who have lost good health, know its value."

We listen silently. It is a beautiful poem, still . . .

Why would my freedom be in jeopardy? I wonder. *I am young. I am healthy. Why should I worry?*

There is a knock at the door. The air suddenly fills with tension.

"Come in, please," our teacher calls, sounding a bit nervous. We stand up straight as the door opens. A middle-aged gentleman, tall, blond, well dressed, enters.

"Boys and girls, this is our guest from the Board of Education, Pan Dombrowski," our teacher announces.

"Good morning, boys and girls."

"Good morning, sir," we answer in one voice.

Our teacher points to her desk chair. "Please, sir, sit here."

"Thank you." He bows politely and sits down.

"Sit down, children." Our teacher smiles as if to assure us that all is well.

My heart beats faster. Is he here to find an excuse to close up a Jewish school?

Our visitor's pale blue eyes take in the classroom. "I see lots of student artwork and poems." He looks pleased. "You seem to be a very creative group."

"They love to do original work," our teacher comments, her voice filled with pride.

Pan Dombrowski's eyes narrow as he looks directly at a boy in the front row. "What is your name?"

The boy stands up. His reddish blond hair falls across his forehead.

"Avrom Meyerowicz, sir," he replies nervously.

"Do you have a Polish name?" Pan Dombrowski's voice sounds harsh.

"My name is Avrom Meyerowicz," Avrom repeats in a firm voice. His cheeks take on color.

Pan Dombrowski makes a face. "You should have a Polish name."

Miss Yoskowicz's voice fills with controlled anger. "Avrom Meyerowicz is a beautiful name." She looks directly at Avrom, her best student. "It is a good name."

Avrom lowers his eyes. "Thank you."

Pan Dombrowski's cool glance stops at Avrom's flushed face. "You may sit down."

Avrom takes a deep breath as he sits down.

"Who are the artists here?" Pan Dombrowski asks, studying the artwork on the classroom walls.

Some students raise their hands.

"Good work." He grins.

High above my desk hangs a framed print.

"Who did this painting?" He turns to Miss Yoskowicz.

"Artist unknown." She smiles, calls on me. "Riva, would you please tell us what you see in this picture?"

My heart beats faster. I am nearsighted and cannot see small details. I try to hide the fact that I need glasses. Kids make fun of those who wear glasses; they call them "four-eyes." In class I take quick notes as the teachers speak. When they write on the blackboard I copy the notes from it after class. I manage. I am a good student.

My head pounds. The picture is too high on the wall for me to see details.

Miss Yoskowicz sounds a bit annoyed. "The class is waiting."

Cold sweat trickles down my neck. I swallow hard. "A beautiful sailboat." My voice trembles slightly. "Its white sails move lightly in the breeze out to the blue open sea. The sun smiles brightly." Silence fills the room.

I continue. I do not see the puzzled faces of my fellow students, my teacher, or our visitor. "Large, white seagulls escort the sailboat, bidding it a safe journey." I take a deep breath, look toward my teacher. Her face flushes as she stares at me.

Pan Dombrowski smiles. "What imagination."

Someone begins to laugh. Others join in. The bell rings. The visitor leaves. I remain sitting, dazed and bewildered.

"We will have to talk," Miss Yoskowicz whispers, then she, too, leaves.

Some students look amused as they pass me. I climb on my desk and stare at the picture. My knees buckle. I lean against the wall. A large bowl of colorful fruit stares back at me from the picture. My cheeks feel hot. I bite my lips and swallow the lump in my throat.

Miss Yoskowicz waits for me outside the classroom. She puts her arms around me, holds me close. "I did not know that you are nearsighted. I did not mean to put you in a position where you had to make up a story rather than admit that you could not see. I am sorry. I will put you in the first row and tell your mother that you need eyeglasses."

My eyes well up with tears.

"It is all right, Riva." Her hand caresses my hair. She grins. "It was funny. You have imagination."

"Will the Board of Education close our school because of me?"

"They would like to find a reason to close all Jewish schools. But Pan Dombrowski had nothing to pick on today. He liked your imagination and was very impressed. I am sure we are safe, for a while." She sighs.

I look up as my uncle Baruch approaches. He is my favorite uncle and my science teacher. All the students adore him. He is Mama's youngest brother, her pride and joy. She helped him through school and Teacher's Seminary. After graduating from The Medem School he started attending a Polish university to study medicine. Only a certain number of Jews were accepted each year. Still, prejudice drove him away and he became a teacher.

"What is wrong, Riva?" He raises my chin.

"I made a fool of myself," I sob.

He looks at Miss Yoskowicz for an explanation.

"Riva needs eyeglasses. I just found out that she is nearsighted."

"Eyeglasses make you look smart." Uncle Baruch puts his hand on my shoulder. "Are you okay to go to your next class or would you rather stay in the teachers' room for a while?" Uncle Baruch asks. His gentle, strong voice calms me.

"I will go to class, Teacher." I never call him Uncle while in school.

"Someday you, too, will be a teacher." He touches my cheek lightly.

"I would like to be a teacher and a writer." I smile through my tears.

"You will be."

The bell rings as I enter Mrs. Melman's class. "I am sorry I am late, Teacher."

She nods. I walk to my seat.

"Riva." Her voice is warm and low. "I think this seat closer to the blackboard will be better for you." She points to an empty seat in the front row. "I made some changes in the class seating."

My heart beats faster as I sit down. I glance sideways at the other students. No one is staring at me. They are listening to Mrs. Melman explain the homework assignment, an essay.

"I will let you pick your own topic. Use your imagination."

Miss Yoskowicz's words echo in my ears. "Our visitor was impressed by your vivid imagination."

I rush home to our two-room apartment on the first floor of a crowded wooden structure housing seventeen families. Ten of us live here: Grandmother Rochl; Mama; my two older sisters, Mala and Chana; my older brother, Yankl; my three younger brothers, Motele, Laibele, Moishele; Tosia, our housekeeper; me.

The factory which Mama and her partner, Gershon, own and operate is in a four-story brick building only a few houses away. A widow with seven children, Mama works long days.

I run into the factory. Men and women work on large sewing machines that make loud buzzing sounds as the fabric is pushed quickly forward. Some women sit at a table finishing garments by hand. They smile at me as I enter.

Mama moves quickly away from the huge table covered with patterns of little girls' coats and puts her arms around me. She kisses my head.

"Glasses will be very becoming. I made an appointment with the eye doctor." She sees my puzzled expression. "Uncle Baruch called. He said you had an emotional day."

"I made a fool of myself. I hope the Board of Education will not close the school because of me." My tears well again.

Mama holds me close to her. It feels good.

I notice a pile of scrap fabric at the end of the cutting table. Mama made a rag doll for me when I was little from scraps of fabric. She would have liked to buy me a store-made doll, with silky hair, pink cheeks, red lips, a pretty dress, but they cost too much. I still love this doll. My eyes light up as I rush home.

"I will let the doll speak for me."

My pen rushes over the paper before me. Pages fill up quickly. Words pour from the depth of my heart.

A deep sigh rips from my chest. My essay is done. I put the pages into a folder for Mrs. Melman.

Several days later I walk into school wearing glasses. My heart beats fast. Will the other children make fun of me?

"You look nice." Genia, my best friend, greets me with a warm smile.

Mrs. Melman, too, grins as she walks toward her desk.

"How are we doing with our essays?" Mrs. Melman's eyes move curiously over the faces of her students. "Is anyone finished?"

I raise my hand.

"Well, Riva, let's hear your essay."

She motions for me to stand in front of her desk as she pulls her chair to the side, watching me as I move slowly toward her.

My voice trembles as I begin to read, softly at first, then louder with feeling.

"'What My Doll Told Me.'"

"My name is Rag Doll. That is the name Riva gave me.

"Before I became Rag Doll I was a large scrap of fabric from little girls' coats, waiting to be sold to the man buying scraps from factories. I do not know what would have become of me.

"The nice lady who runs the factory, Pani Minska, took me out of the pile in the large box near the cutting table. Her hands were soft and warm. Her blue eyes had a strange twinkle as she whispered to herself: 'Such pretty fabric, I will make a doll for Riva. Mala and Chana are too big for dolls. My poor children have to work to help support the family; Mala and Chana in a weaving factory, Yankl in the tailor shop. Such a heavy burden for teenagers. Riva is still a child. She needs a doll to play with just like other little girls. I wish I had the money to buy one of the pretty dolls that fill the store windows, but food comes first.'

"She smiles. 'In the Jewish folktale "The Golem," a giant made of clay sprang to life. I will make a doll from rags. Maybe it, too, will spring to life and bring joy to my child.'

"Her fingers move quickly. 'I have to return to my work. I have seven young children to support. It is the busy season. Loans, made when there is little work, must be paid. When the season is over I will have to borrow again, to pay for food, to pay the rent, to pay for the children's schooling. I know that Moishe, the grocer, inflates my bills when I buy on credit. But he lets me buy on credit until I have the money to pay the bills.'

"Her warm fingers stuff my body with cotton. Button eyes, a

painted nose and lips bring me to life. As she puts a newly made cotton dress on my plump body, her eyes shine bright. 'It is made with love,' she whispers. 'If I could only make some playthings for Motele, Laibele, and Moishele. What toys can I make for little boys using rags?' She thinks for a moment. 'Stuffed dogs, stuffed cats,' she calls out happily. 'I can make stuffed animals. But where do I get the time? So much work, so little time.' Tears flow from her eyes. 'I wish their mother did not have to work for a living.' She wipes her eyes quickly. 'I must work. I will not take charity. I will not send my children to an orphanage. My dear husband loved his children. He died so young. I must be the mother and father, give them love for both of us. My children are the joy of my life. A smile, a hug, a kiss from my children brings sunshine into my life.'

"She holds me close to her as if I were one of her children. 'Someday life will be easier. Someday.' Her lips form a smile as she whispers, 'As long as there is life, there is hope.'"

I take a deep breath as I read the last line, Mama's favorite saying: "'As long as there is life, there is hope.'"

I look at Mrs. Melman. She wipes her eyes with a white handkerchief. The silence is suddenly broken by thunderous applause.

My face feels hot. My classmates are all standing, clapping with all their might. "Bravo, Riva, bravo."

Mrs. Melman puts her arm around my shoulders. Her voice quivers. "You must read this to all the other classes."

Several classes are put together for a special program. Cold sweat trickles down my back. I am the special program today.

My body trembles as I notice Pan Dombrowski enter the room. He nods and sits down. My uncle smiles at me from the back of the room. The story is about Mama, his beloved sister. Will he be upset that I put her struggle on paper? I speak of her love and devotion. That should please him. I take a deep breath and read.

"Bravo, Riva." Uncle Baruch holds me in his strong arms. I hear the applause from students and teachers. "I am proud of you. My sister will be proud of you. A writer was born today."

His eyes glow with pride. "Mr. Dombrowski, too, seems touched," he whispers. "Maybe for a while he will leave us in peace."

Later, Mama reads the essay surrounded by her children. She holds me in her arms, looks lovingly around her, and whispers, "My blessings. My blessings."

Interview ∽ RUTH MINSKY SENDER

Where did you get your idea for "The Rag Doll"?
I wrote a story in Yiddish when I was ten years old about my rag doll. When I was asked to submit a story I decided to write about the rag doll because the story of my childhood, my Jewish school, and living with anti-Semitism was always with me.

Then you are Riva? And the rag doll was real?
I am Riva. I left the rag doll in the Lodz ghetto when we were deported to Auschwitz. I came back to my home after liberation, but the Polish woman to whom our apartment was given did not let me into the house. I have no traces of my childhood.

In spite of the obvious anti-Semitism Riva observes all around her, your story is filled with gentle, loving people and ends on a note of triumph. Can you comment on that?
The people in my life were my shield against prejudice. They brought out the good in all people. I want young people to learn to be proud of their heritage and learn what hate, prejudice, and indifference lead to. Mama, Motele, Laibele, Moishele, Uncle Baruch, many members of my family, all of my teachers, and most of my classmates perished during the Holocaust.

I survived. I write. I teach. I lecture. I must not let them be forgotten. They had names, they had hopes, they had dreams. Mama's legacy, "As long as there is life, there is hope," helped me hold on to life when it would have been easier to give up.

Biography — RUTH MINSKY SENDER

Born in Lodz, Poland, Ruth Minsky Sender came to the United States in 1950. "Even as a child," she says, "I always wanted to teach and write. I wrote poems even in the Nazi death camps. They helped me to hold on to hope, to life." Her books *The Cage* and *To Life* are based on her own experiences during the Holocaust. She has been honored with the Merit of Distinction Citation from the International Center for Holocaust Studies and the Major Joseph H. Lief J.W.V. Brotherhood Award. Her books have been cited as Notable Children's Trade Books in the Field of Social Studies, a Notable Children's Trade Book for Language Arts, and a New York Public Library Book for the Teen Age. *The Holocaust Lady* draws on her visits to schools to speak about her experiences.

Frank and Stein

by Eve B. Feldman

Dear *Frank*,

I hate you. Don't take it personally. Right now, there are more things in my life I hate than I like. Sorry, will explain myself later. I hear Sidney coming, and I don't want her to know about this.

Dear Frank,

It's me again. I guess I should introduce myself. (I can't believe I'm doing this.) Formally, my name is Benjamin Stein. Okay, Benjamin Milton Stein. My family calls me Benjy. Kids in school call me Stein.

You probably didn't even know you had a name. I gave it to you. See, some person I don't know, some great-aunt of my mom's sent you as a Bar Mitzvah gift because she's not coming. You are not the worst gift I've gotten. It's sort of a three-way tie between you, cuff links with my initials on them, and some nine-hundred-pound book in Hebrew. (Some relative in Israel sent that with someone who was coming to the United States, and my parents and I had to drive to some stranger's house to pick up the gift that came "all the way from Israel.") This book is huge and I can't understand it. Sure I studied Hebrew in Hebrew school and have learned my part for my Bar Mitzvah. But a whole book in Hebrew? Who are we kidding here? The words don't even have vowels in them! You are supposed to figure out what it says by the letters that are in it and the context.

"Context" is a big word this year. My English teacher is drilling it into us. She's big on vocabulary. That's really why you have your name.

"Frank" was one of our vocabulary words. You know, "frank," meaning "honest" or "open." So when I opened you up, it just popped into my head: If I actually wrote something in a diary, it should be frank. Explain more later.

Benjy, aka Stein

Dear Frank,

I forgot to explain about Sidney. She's almost seven and annoying. When I saw you, I said, "I don't want a dumb diary."

Sidney said, "I like it. I want a diary. Can I have it, Mom, please, please, please, pretty please?"

"It has my initials, not yours," I reminded her.

"I don't care. It's soft and I could write down a whole book in it maybe." She was stroking the leather the whole time, as if it were some kind of pet.

I guess it was mean, but I didn't want her to have my Bar Mitzvah gift. I'm the one who is studying my Torah portion. I'm the one who has to write a speech and stand up in front of all those people, including my friends and even the girls who are coming. So I didn't feel like sharing, and I said, "Never mind. I'll keep it."

I took you upstairs and buried you in my sock drawer. And then I just decided to try writing and well, uh-oh, Sidney is coming.

Frank,

Sidney didn't find you. I hid you, so fast. That made me think about something else I should tell you. It's hard, but here goes.

There is probably another reason I am writing to you. We had to read a diary in Hebrew school. It's probably the most famous diary in the world, and it was written by someone about my age—except a girl. Her name is Anne Frank. I guess I should say it was Anne Frank. She was hiding in an atticlike place, hiding from the Nazis with her family. She just wrote down what happened every day and her thoughts. Parts of it are funny and parts of it are scary, but it is really, really, really sad. I cried in my head about it. I mean I managed to keep the tears inside my eyes, but they were still there. I think that is maybe the other reason I named you. Anne named her diary, and I named you. I think I chose "frank" for honesty, but maybe it was for her, too. I don't want to write more about this or think about it. So, later.

Hey, Frank,

This Bar Mitzvah stuff is making me crazy. My mother and father can't seem to talk or think about anything else. My mother has these weird phone calls all day. The band. The caterer. The balloon lady. The photographer. See, it's a custom. If you are a Jewish boy, when you turn thirteen you go to temple and read from the Torah. And you make a speech and then your family celebrates. They throw a party. Everyone is invited—friends, family, people I never heard of. Lots of those. Take yesterday, six replies came back.

"So who are Barney and Louise Mitchell?"

"People from Dad's business."

"I never heard of them," I said.

"Maybe they never heard of you either," said Sidney, dancing around the table.

"Butt out," I warned her.

"It's an occasion," said my mother. "We want to celebrate and invite all kinds of people."

"I think we should invite more of my friends, too," said Sidney.

I rolled my eyes and Sidney got mad, and we sort of chased each other around the house till my mom ran out of patience. (Okay, I accidentally knocked over a vase, but I caught it before it broke.)

Stein

Dear Frank,

Another gift came in the mail. I fell over laughing. It is a shaving kit. Me, shaving? Hah! What I really want as a Bar Mitzvah gift is a golden retriever. Not getting one. Sidney is allergic.

Frank,

Went to Jason P.'s Bar Mitzvah, and the party was at night in a country club, and it was so fancy. It was hard to tell who were the guests and who were the waiters, because they all wore tuxedoes. Mom asked me to describe everything.

Like: "What was the centerpiece?"

Me: "What?"

Mom: "Decorations in the middle of the table?"

Me: "Every table was a different football team with all kinds of things from that team." I suddenly realized that Jason had a theme—football. Andrew had a theme—bikes.

Me: "Mom, we forgot to find me a theme."

Mom: (Laughing) "Not really."

Me: "You picked a theme without asking me?"

Mom: "Your theme is 'Bar Mitzvah.'"

Me: "Funny one, Ma. Everyone's theme is Bar Mitzvah!"

Mom: "Yes, but we're not going to cover it up with other themes. We're trying to keep it simple and warm."

I started worrying a lot. What if this Bar Mitzvah is so unlike all the others that my friends make fun of me? Well, maybe not Zane, he doesn't say mean stuff, but everyone else and people I barely know and girls. There are girls coming to my Bar Mitzvah, including one whose name I won't write down in case this falls into the wrong hands, but trust me, she is cute. And I wouldn't want her to think I come from a family that does everything wrong.

Me: "We're still having a band and all?"

Mom: "Of course. Stop worrying, it will be great."

Problem: What if Mom's idea of great and my idea of great don't match? Mom likes marmalade.

A worried Stein

Frank,

I am writing this under the covers, with a flashlight. That's why this may look like someone else's handwriting. But it is still me. Or maybe this is the new me, the me WHO IS GOING TO CANCEL HIS BAR MITZVAH. Yep, you heard it first, loud and clear. I have two major reasons. Two great reasons:

1. The minute you get bar mitzvahed, you become a man, according to Jewish tradition. I am not interested in that deal at this moment. It doesn't look like a fun thing, which is sort of related to reason two.

2. If we cancel this thing, my parents will save a lot of money. See, tonight I overheard my parents:

Dad: "Eileen, what are these balloons going to be made out of? Gold?"

Mom: "Lower your voice, Howard, you'll wake the children. And trust me, this is the lowest price. You should have heard what they wanted for flowers."

Dad: "You know, this whole thing is getting out of hand. It's like we're dealing with Monopoly money. Real money is not so easy to earn, you know."

Mom: "I know, believe me I know, and I am cutting corners left and right."

See, Frank, when I am a man, I will have to make money to support my family, like my mom and dad. And that's scary. What if I have a bunch of kids and have to make a zillion Bar and Bat Mitzvahs? There is only one thing to do: We cancel mine, and then my parents don't have to pay for it, and I don't have to become a man, overnight, since I'm not ready and all. If I don't cancel, I'll probably have to go to work immediately.

B.

Dear Frank,

At breakfast, I suggested we cancel my Bar Mitzvah, or at least postpone it indefinitely. My parents laughed. Dad actually spat out his orange juice and had to change his shirt.

Ben

Dear Frank,

Discussed the situation with Grandpa. He listened intently when I told him I was thinking of calling the whole thing off. Then when I explained why, he burst out laughing. (Somehow everybody but me is laughing.)

"You won't need to go to work so fast, Benjy," he said between hearty ha-ha's. "Your parents make enough of a living to afford this and besides you'll get presents. From me, too, and trust me, they will eat up a big chunk of the costs. Big chunk. So don't worry, all you have to do is learn your part."

I felt better, but learning my part is not so simple, either. Not only do I have to read this thing in a whole other language, but I have to chant it—sing it this way here and that way there. Singing is not my best thing. And I have regular homework, too. A social studies test and I'm in advanced math and it's tricky. And English—we're reading Shakespeare, *Julius Caesar.* Today in school, Matt said, "Mrs. K., are you sure this is English? It sounds weird." I thought, Yeah, try reading Hebrew.

Benjy

P.S. Grandpa called me last night and said he forgot to tell me something. Seems we have a whole bunch of ancestors who had to have Bar Mitzvahs late because of persecution in Europe, pogroms, fleeing the Nazis, even one cousin of Grandpa's who had his Bar Mitzvah as an adult in Israel after years in a concentration camp. Pretty scary stuff. After I got off the phone, Dad noticed that I was sort of sad. I asked him if he knew about these people in our family.

Dad took me to the attic and dug up an old family tree. Boy, with all those branches, I figured we must have some famous relative out there somewhere, but there didn't seem to be any. Dad showed me some tattered photo albums of all these people who are somehow related to me, cousins of nieces or brothers of uncles—men with long beards and stuff!

"This," said my father, "is a bit of your, our, family history. And Grandpa told you the truth. Not everyone could just study freely and go to temple and celebrate our tradition."

"So like I have to carry all this weight on my shoulders for everyone who had it rougher?"

Dad laughed. "Benjy, maybe becoming a man in the Jewish tradition means that, too."

Frank, I am so worn out from thinking about this that I can't keep on writing. If I don't finish my homework and go to sleep, by tomorrow I may look yellow and withered, like the pictures in those albums.

Hey, Frank,

Lizzie, who has been my friend since nursery school, told me that all the girls are talking about what they'll wear to my Bar Mitzvah. It is only the third one of the year, so I guess they are still not sure what to wear. Didn't realize girl guests have more problems than boy guests. (We have to wear a suit or sports jacket, and a tie.) Question: After my Bar Mitzvah, if I really am a man, does that mean I'll figure out how to tie a tie myself?

Gee, Frank, I wish you could write back.

Benjy

Frank,

Have Sidney problems:

1. She is going to get called up to the *bimah*. That's the part of the temple where the rabbi and the cantor and I stand for the Bar Mitzvah. And anyone who is in the service gets called up. So Sidney is prancing around the house singing one of the prayers from services—"*Adon olam, asher malach.*" She's dancing and twirling around while singing. I reminded her that she can't do that in temple. "You have to be still and calm and sedate," I said.

"That's good," said Sidney. "They named a word for me, 'Sid-ate' is for Sidney!" My parents laughed. They think she is adorable. Sometimes she is, but at my Bar Mitzvah, I can't afford to be embarrassed. There will be all kinds of people my age there, including girls.

2. I think Sidney has worked out some kind of surprise for the party

part. I heard her say to my mother, "Tell me again how I know when it's my turn." That's when I walked into the kitchen, and my mother said, "Sidney, if you get ready for your bath, we'll have time to read you a book." I could tell Mom was trying to switch subjects fast. So I hatched a plan of my own and volunteered to read to Sidney.

"Don't you have too much homework?" my mother asked. "And have you finished writing your Bar Mitzvah speech?" (Aha, I thought, she is trying to keep us apart so I won't ask Sidney about the plan.)

"No, I'm fine," I said.

So I ended up reading her one of her *Russell and Elisa* books, which I actually like myself. They used to be mine anyway. And I pumped her for information.

"So do you want to sing a song or something at my party?"

"It's all . . ." She stopped midsentence and gave me a big fake yawn. "I am so tired, Benjy. I want to go to sleep." She yawned again. Pretty good acting, actually. But I still think she is up to something. She has two favorite songs—"Little Rabbit Foo Foo" and "Miss Lucy Had a Baby." Either one would be EMBARRASSING.

Ugh, more things to worry about. And now I still have the work my mother mentioned. I'm yawning, too. Bye, Frank.

Benjy

Dear Frank,

Getting closer. Met with the cantor and had to chant my haftorah. I was so nervous, I thought I might pass out. He always seemed nice in temple, but that was from a distance. Up close, I could see little things like a long hair sticking out from the edge of his eyebrow. It was distracting, but I had to concentrate on doing my stuff right.

"Not bad. You still have time to work on it. Practice slowing down. Do it louder. Remember the trop." (Those are the marks that tell you how to chant. Would you believe people have been doing this for thousands and thousands of years?)

My mother is calling me. Bet it's Bar Mitzvah related. What now?

B

Hey, Frank,

Mom wanted to talk about two terrible words—"candle lighting." See, at the party, they wheel out your cake, and it has candles on it and you call up people to light them. It is an honor to get called up. So who gets called? Some people are obvious: my grandparents, Uncle Jack and Aunt Jann, my parents and Sidney, Uncle Ron and his family, our neighbors, the Richardsons, my dad's great-aunt Gertie, but Mom wants to know which of my friends get called. If I mention some but not all, will they hate me? Who started this dopey custom anyway? I tried to suggest no candle lighting, but Mom was persistent.

Stein in trouble

Dear Frank,

Just when you think the pressure is at the top, it goes up like a runaway balloon. My mother has made up poems for everyone at the candle lighting! Like "This aunt is truly great and not just because she's almost eighty-eight!"

This stuff is so corny, and I'm supposed to read it! Oh, boy, I am going to be the laughingstock of the seventh grade. I'll probably be so nervous that I'll drop a candle and everything will catch on fire.

Frank, there are just two more days and I'm not sure I can make it.

Frank,

Survived "rehearsal." Didn't actually have to open my mouth, which was good because it was stuck shut like glue. We just had to move around and practice who does what and when, including the loudest version of *Adon Olam* ever sung by a human being under seven feet tall. If I knew what Sidney has planned for the party, I'd probably stay home. We learned about probability in math. What is the probability that I will survive this experience without catching on fire or just embarrassing myself to death? Answer: my new favorite number—zero.

Frank,

It's Friday morning, about 4:30 A.M. The last time I woke up this early, I had a 101-degree fever and threw up on the way to the bathroom. I feel sick all right, but not with fever. I had the most awful nightmare. I was in temple, in my Bar Mitzvah suit. When I got up to chant, all that came out was weird stuff, like, "Fuzzy Wuzzy was a bear. Fuzzy Wuzzy had no hair. Fuzzy Wuzzy wasn't fuzzy, was he?" My Bar Mitzvah speech, where I thank the rabbi, the cantor, my parents, and my teachers, came out: "How much wood would a woodchuck chuck if a woodchuck would chuck wood?"

If only I could hire someone to double for me, a stunt man. If and when I do become a man, I will start that as a business. Rent a Bar Mitzvah double. I'll be rich in five minutes. Frank, I'm not scared anymore, I AM TOTALLY TERRIFIED. Zane told me his cousin Harry fainted right in the middle of his Bar Mitzvah. I'll be lucky if that's all I do. Fuzzy Wuzzy.

F.

It's over. It was unbelievable. I made a mistake or two chanting, but no one seemed to notice. The rabbi and cantor praised me and shook my hand, and then everything was a blur. Didn't drop candles. Did do limbo. Sidney sang a homemade song about how I am a great brother! YOU KNOW WHO came up to me right afterward and said, "Your sister is adorable, and you must be one great brother." And she called me Ben, not Stein. Everyone seemed to have fun. Even Dad and Mom— they danced and hugged and looked proud and happy. Frank, you won't believe this, but it was the best day of my life. If this is what it's like to be a man, I think I can handle that, too. Wish you could have been there.

Benjamin Milton Stein

Interview ∽ EVE B. FELDMAN

Learning Hebrew looms large in Benjy's story. Was it important in your own life?

My father was from Russia/Poland and his parents sent him to the Hebrew University in Jerusalem to study. (There were quotas on Jewish students in Polish universities and the rumblings that would lead to the horrors of World War II.) When he arrived in the United States from Palestine, his uncle introduced him to my mother, "an American girl who spoke Hebrew." So these two people, from opposite sides of the earth, were connected because they could speak the same language. They were engaged within days and married within weeks.

So Hebrew was spoken in your home?

My parents spoke Hebrew to each other as a secret language of communication. The only words I knew were *ema* (mother), *aba* (father), *tapooach* (apple), and one complete sentence, *Ani rotza kelev*. I thought if I asked for a dog in Hebrew, I'd get one!

Despite all the strong observance of Judaism in my home, I was a Hebrew school dropout. My brother and sister were bar and bat mitzvahed. I somehow had the misfortune to be in a class of wild boys who spent the class time fooling around and teachers who quit after a few weeks. I finally refused to attend, but I actually became ardently involved in Jewish tradition from my summers. I spent years at a wonderful old Jewish camp, Cejwin, where I took to the folk dancing and prayers like a duck to water.

We had relatives in Israel who visited occasionally throughout my childhood. One of these, a cousin my age, is captured in my novel *Seymour, the Formerly Fearful*, and it was he who convinced me that I should come to Israel, but not as a tourist. So as an adult, after college and graduate school, I went to Israel, enrolled in an *ulpan*, and set out to learn Hebrew. My cousin introduced me to an eligible Israeli who was studying engineering with him. I loved Israel, Hebrew, and my own special Israeli. It is ironic that the Hebrew school dropout in the family lived in Israel for eight years, married an Israeli, and is fluent in Hebrew.

Did the idea for "Frank and Stein" grow out of your own experiences?

While I was thinking about what kind of story to write, my nephew was preparing for his Bar Mitzvah and received monogrammed cuff links from someone who could not attend the Bar Mitzvah. I suddenly came up with the idea of a boy who receives a monogrammed diary as an unwanted Bar Mitzvah gift. The name of the boy came to me as I was falling asleep, and I realized the story would be "Frank, the diary" and "Stein, the boy."

I can recognize parts of me in each of the characters. I can see myself in Benjamin Stein (writer, worrier, person who learned Hebrew and marveled at it); in Benjamin's mother (good humored, trying to plan a tasteful, unadorned Bar Mitzvah party); in Sidney (the sister who watches the gifts her brother doesn't appreciate and wishes they were hers); and in the grandfather and father who appreciate the connection to ancestors and tradition.

Tell us more about that connection and your feelings about it.

I once heard an anecdote that expresses my feelings about my Jewish heritage. Imagine that someone in your family came to you with a locked box and said, "This box has been in our family for centuries and contains family treasures used by each generation of our family. I am giving it to you to take care of and pass on to the next generation, just as I am passing it on to you."

Now imagine that in that box were all kinds of large and small items, some of which would not appear valuable to the naked eye, but you knew that your parents and grandparents and great-grandparents had not only owned these same items, but had used them in their daily lives, in times of joy and in times of sorrow. Wouldn't you want to keep these things, just for the link they represented with all your ancestors? And imagine if those items stretched back over five thousand years!

This is a metaphor for the riches of the Jewish tradition—the rituals, the laws, the customs. I feel these are prized possessions to be treasured, examined, and then shared. (I think that every cultural heritage should be explored and shared with new generations.) Maybe it's through language, music, art, literature, or religion, but there are so many ways to explore a culture's rich heritage and feel connected to the past and be the link that joins that past to the future.

Biography ⟋ EVE B. FELDMAN

As a child, Eve B. Feldman was a "ravenous bookworm." She says, "My major worry was how to live long enough to read every single book in the library! In college I decided to become a teacher with a kind of evangelical wish to spread my enthusiasm for learning. And that same passion took me back to writing books for children." With degrees from Sarah Lawrence College and Harvard Graduate School of Education, she has taught elementary school, English as a second language, and remedial reading. Her books include *Animals Don't Wear Pajamas,* an *American Bookseller* "Pick of the Lists" and NSTA-CBC Outstanding Science Trade Book for Children; *That Cat!,* a Child Study Children's Book Committee Best Book of the Year; *Dog Crazy,* a nominee for the Florida State Sunshine Award; and *Birthdays!: Celebrating Life Around the World,* a winner of the 1997 *Early Childhood News* Director's Choice Award. Ms. Feldman and her husband have two sons.

Wrestling with Angels

by Carol Matas

It has me pinned to the ground. I can't move. It wants me to surrender. I try to catch my breath—it is coming in ragged gasps. I try to think. And then I see a weakness, or I feel one. I can still move my trunk even though my legs and arms are caught tight. I wait, gather my strength, pretend to acquiesce. And then I move from the waist, the hip, thrusting to my right. It is surprised. I wrench my arms free and we tumble over each other, over and over, its sweet breath almost suffocating me until suddenly I am on top, pinning it down.

"Release me," it says.

"No!"

"I will bless you, if you release me."

I laugh. "Bless me and kill me!"

"Release me."

"What kind of blessing?" I ask.

"I will bless you."

"Jaci! Wake up. You'll be late for school."

I sat up in bed with a start. For a split second I had no idea where I was, who I was, I'd been so deep in the dream. "Wow," I murmured. "That was a truly weird dream." So real, too. Like it had happened. More real than sitting in that bed.

When I swung my legs over the side onto the floor, I had a terrible twinge in my right hip. I grabbed the spot. It hurt! And I was covered in sweat, as if I'd actually been fighting. I shook my head. I'd never had a dream like that before—clearer and more vivid than life.

"Jaci. Hurry! The bus'll be here in twenty minutes."

Twenty minutes! It took me that long just to shower. And Mr. Greeler, my English teacher, hates it when we're late. We have so little time, you see. Because we're at a Hebrew day school we have the morning to do what kids at the regular high school take a full day to do. And in the afternoon we learn Hebrew, Torah, all that stuff.

Somehow I managed to catch the bus, with wet hair, no breakfast, cranky, and a little disoriented. My fourteenth birthday was coming up in a week and I was going to do two things to mark the occasion: Becky, my best friend, was arranging for us to get a ride downtown so I could pierce something—I wasn't sure what, yet. And I was finally about to agree to go out with Josh. I'm the only one of all my girl-friends who hasn't pierced *something* and who's never had a boyfriend. I've been feeling kind of uncomfortable lately when I'm with them. You know, time to get with the program—I hardly have anything to talk to them about because they're always gabbing about boys and their latest piercing. It's not that they're *pressuring* me or anything, but if I want to be with them we have to have the same interests—right?

The dream I'd had was so vivid that instead of fading away like they usually do it stayed with me all morning. In fact, it wasn't even like a normal dream. By the end of the morning, when Isaac and I were working on a Torah study together, it was stronger rather than weaker. I couldn't concentrate. Isaac got irritated.

Isaac is from an observant home. Because there's only one Jewish day school in the city, Isaac is forced to go to a school made up mostly of non-Orthodox kids. You can tell he hates it—obviously the rest of us aren't good enough for him. He and the other Orthodox kids treat us as if we aren't even really Jewish—it's *their* way, *their* rules, or no way. And *I* had to get stuck with him on this project.

Since I wasn't concentrating at all he snapped at me. "What's your problem?"

Then, I don't know why I did it, except that the dream was *so* overwhelming and I just had to talk about it, and he did ask. . . . I told him my dream.

He stared at me for a moment before he spoke. At first I thought he was so stunned I'd said anything personal to him that he *couldn't* speak. But it wasn't that at all.

"You were wrestling with the divine, just like your namesake," he said, finally.

"Huh?" Brilliant comeback.

"Jacob. I guess that's what your parents were thinking when they named you Jaci, spelled that way."

"Jacob," I repeated. "So?"

"You know the story. In Genesis. Jacob wrestles with a divine being. He asks for the being to bless him. The being blesses him and gives him the name Israel, from whom we are all descended."

"Oh," I sighed. "That explains it. It must have been stuck in my subconscious somewhere."

"Maybe," Isaac said.

Isaac is actually *very* good looking, and my friends and I think it's a shame he's such a snob. Black hair, blue eyes—*huge* blue eyes—no zits, broad shoulders . . . He stared at me intensely with a thoughtful look on his face.

"Maybe it was real," he said.

I burst out laughing. "Yeah, right."

His face flushed but he didn't back down.

"It could have been real. Maybe you were visited by an angel."

"Oh, sure."

"It's possible."

"No, it isn't."

"Yes, it is."

"Fine," I said, realizing I was getting nowhere. "Why?"

"Do I look like the Almighty?" he replied.

"No!"

"Then I wouldn't know why, would I?"

The time for work on our project ended and Mr. Rubin began a discussion on Job. On why people suffer. Job was a good man. But God did all these terrible things to him on a bet with Satan—a bet that Job would stay faithful. God won. I can tell you, I wouldn't have reacted like Job. I would have cursed God. But then, you have to believe in God to curse God. What kind of God would let the Holocaust happen?

Still, that dream wouldn't let go of me. Could there be any truth to what Isaac had said? I didn't see how. Dreams come out of our minds. That's it, isn't it?

After class I was walking down the hall and a woman stopped me. Our school is part of the Jewish Community Center and there are people here all day, for meetings, classes, everything. She put her hand on my arm and said, "Mystery. The universe is mysterious." And then she walked away.

I looked to see if any of my friends were around. I saw Becky up ahead. "Becky," I called, "wait up. Look, see that woman . . ." But she was gone.

"What?" Becky asked.

"This woman stopped me," I said. I repeated what she said.

Becky laughed. "I'm telling you, there are more people around here who are crazy than there are normal ones! The other day some old guy asked me if I could find him a used car. I mean, do I look like a used car dealer?" She shook her head. "So? All set? What're you going to get done? Eyebrow? Nose? Belly button?"

"I'm not sure," I replied. "You tell me." I didn't want to suggest something she'd think was stupid.

"You don't seem that keen."

"No, I am, just . . . just . . . strange things have been happening."

"C'mon, let's go eat."

Lunch was the usual. We met just outside the cafeteria; me, Becky, Sue, Sarah, Corry, and Robin. Becky had a nose stud, Sue an eyebrow ring, Sarah a nose ring, Corry had pierced her belly button; so had

Robin. Robin's was infected and she was on antibiotics. Her parents *freaked* when they found out. Actually *all* the parents were totally grossed out except Sarah's. Her mom wants to get *her* nose pierced. Now *that's* gross.

Over lunch, the girls all had advice about which piercing would suit me best. Then they talked about their boyfriends and where they were all going this weekend and just how *far* things were going. And how I just *had* to get together with Josh because he was too cute. I felt out of it, not part of the group—I'd noticed that more and more over the last couple months. I hardly said a word and I realized that they might not even miss me if I weren't there.

"Jaci! Earth to Jaci!" It was Becky.

"Yeah?"

"Time for ethics class. Come on."

On my way to ethics I had a terrible thought—*did* I really want to get something pierced? I'd just assumed I *had* to. And yet when I thought about it specifically—nose, belly button . . . Ugh. My stomach twisted up.

Ethics. That class could have been on *anything*. Strange coincidence that it just happened to be on the Jewish approach to our bodies. There was a discussion in class over the concept of returning your body in good shape to God when you are done with it. In other words, no mutilation. So in the middle of class, I blurted this out:

"If you don't believe in God, then you don't have to follow any of these Jewish laws. Correct?"

Ms. Cohen stared at me. The class grew silent for a moment.

Slowly she answered. "Jaci, there are many kinds of Jews. You know that."

"Yes," I said. "I do, of course I do. And I'm not saying I'm not Jewish. I am. But *why* am I?" I stopped. And then I blurted *this* out: "Or maybe I'm not. I mean, if I don't believe in God, and I don't believe in following any of the laws, what's Jewish about me?"

"The Nazis would say you're Jewish," Josh said. Josh is big on anti-Semitism. He thinks the next Holocaust is just around the corner.

"Maybe they would," I answered. "But is that a good enough reason for me to obey all of God's laws? How many of us do anyway? Most people here don't keep the Sabbath, or keep kosher."

Isaac spoke then.

"You have to ask yourself what it means to be a Jew. What is the essence?"

I couldn't help but think how cute he was. Shallow reaction? I guess. It's just that I'd never really taken him seriously before. Or, that is, maybe I'd never felt he'd taken *me* seriously before. Suddenly he was. He seemed to want to engage in a discussion.

Actually, I had never thought about what the essence of being Jewish was. Ms. Cohen looked relieved. "There's our assignment for tomorrow," she said. "Find out. Bring it in. Be prepared."

After class I found Becky. "Listen," I said. "Can't go. Too much homework. We'll do it on the weekend, okay?"

It didn't look all that okay to Becky. Her lips pursed up the way they do when she's mad. I turned and ran for the door before she could say anything.

Josh sat beside me on the bus on the way home. "What made you ask that?" he said.

"I don't know," I admitted. "I didn't even know I was thinking it."

He squeezed my hand. Josh is thin and wiry, with curly brown hair and almost black eyes. He's full of energy. And he's funny, too. When he's not being paranoid. "What's going on? Something bothering you?"

I shook my head. "No," I answered. "I guess not." I don't know why I could tell Isaac about my dream and not Josh.

That made me wonder—why would I want to go out with Josh if I was afraid to tell him about a dream, afraid he'd laugh at me. Maybe having him as a boyfriend wasn't such a great idea after all. But I *had* to if I wanted to stay friends with the girls. I knew that. I sighed.

"You don't sound too happy to me," he said.

"I'm okay," I said.

But was I? I was having all kinds of strange thoughts.

I went home and pulled out all my parents' books. They have a huge library of Judaica. After hours of work I felt like I had some answers. And they surprised me.

I had just closed my eyes after falling into bed when Mom called me. "Phone, darling!"

I picked up, expecting Josh. I knew he'd been at a theater class and lately he's taken to calling just before bed.

"Jaci?"

"Yes."

"It's Isaac."

"Oh. Hi."

"Hi. I was thinking about your dream."

I was embarrassed. "I shouldn't have told you. It was just a stupid dream. Probably all about sex."

Then I stopped and turned beet red. I mean, not the sort of thing you say to a boy you don't know well—especially if he's Orthodox.

"If you were a shrink you'd definitely say that," was his answer. Could have knocked me over with a feather. He wasn't embarrassed at all. "But in the mystical tradition, well, just in Torah study . . ." He paused.

"Go on."

"Are you interested? I don't want to intrude if I'm not welcome."

"Go ahead," I said. "Butt in all you want."

He laughed. "You see, wrestling with a divine being represents wrestling with God, which is what Jews are meant to do. We are meant to argue with God. Maybe the dream had two levels. You are arguing with yourself about certain things. And . . ."

"Yes?"

"You really had a vision. A holy visitation. It happens all the time. It could happen to you."

I was feeling very uncomfortable about the way the conversation was going.

"But why *would* it happen to me?"

"Maybe you're at some kind of crossroads in your life. Maybe God felt it was time to show you the way."

"Whatever."

Isaac paused. "I'm sure that sounds silly to you."

"More like crazy," I said. I was upset. And I didn't care if I hurt his feelings.

"Okay. Crazy." He wasn't mad at me. He paused. "I'm not a weirdo, you know."

That stopped me in my tracks. It's so embarrassing when people know what you're thinking and call you on it.

"I never said you were."

"But you avoid me like I'm going to infect you or something."

"Because you act like the rest of the nonreligious world is scum," I said, deciding to be honest with him. "You're so much better than me, right, because you follow all the commandments."

There was silence on the other end. "You're right," he admitted. "It's easy to feel that way. In fact, since you talked to me this morning I feel like everything I believed in has turned upside down. Because I *did* think anyone who wasn't Orthodox wasn't as good. But God sent you a vision. So you *must* be as good. *Better.* Because He's never sent me one." He sounded wistful.

"God didn't speak to me either. I told you—"

He interrupted me. "Do you *really* believe that?"

I had to tell the truth to him. I don't know why. A truth I didn't even want to admit to myself. "It was—it was like nothing I've ever—experienced. So real. So different." I paused. "It's got me all confused. Things I took for granted this morning I'm not sure of anymore tonight. Like I was going to get something pierced. It never occurred to me *not* to. It was my turn, all my friends have done it. But now—"

"Now you realize you can *choose*," he said.

"Jaci. Bed." Mom again.

"I have to go," I said. "Thanks for calling."

"Thanks for . . . talking," he said. And he hung up quickly. And I knew, all at once, that his "I am better than you" thing was a put-on, that he was insecure around our group, that he cared what *I* thought of him and that he was really embarrassed by his last line. Thanks for talking. Geeky.

I am swimming in a large pool. When I get out children are singing. It is a beautiful song, all in Hebrew. So beautiful I want to cry.

"Jaci!"

Again I sat up in bed, this time trying to figure out the song. Strange thing . . . in the dream I knew all the words. Awake I was sure I'd never heard that song before. I considered the idea that I was going crazy.

In Torah class we talked about Job again. Mr. Rubin discussed the argument Job had with God. And the ending. The mystery of God's will. Isn't that what that woman had said? Mystery. We will never know why God does what God does. Mystery.

I went to ethics. And there I put forth what I had found to be the essence of Judaism.

"'Love your neighbor as yourself.' It's from Leviticus," I said. "And Rabbi Akiva, who was a great scholar, said *that* was it. So, I suppose, God doesn't enter into it. It's a person-to-person thing."

I sat down. Isaac stood up.

"Where does love come from?" he said. "From God," he answered. "God comes into everything."

Everyone started to argue then. Josh, of course, said, "Where was God in the concentration camps?"

And Isaac said, "God didn't make the camps, men did. Free will."

And Becky said, "If God created the world like that, God did an *awful* job."

And Sylvia said, "God isn't a thing. A person. It is an unknown. A vast unknowable thing."

"Yes!" said Isaac. "And Job *never* thought God was punishing him. He knew better. In fact," Isaac continued, "God punishes Job's friends at the end, for insisting that Job was being punished for his sins. A lot of Orthodox people believe the Jews were being punished by God during the Holocaust." He glanced at me then. "I can't believe that."

"I'm glad you can't," Josh exclaimed. "But still—if God could part the Red Sea, why couldn't God destroy the camps? See? If you take one thing literally, you have to take it *all* literally."

"But you can't take it literally," I heard myself saying. "Because it's a mystery."

Josh got mad. "That's so convenient. Say it's a mystery. Say we can't understand! That just lets God off the hook!"

"But what if God was never *on* the hook?" I asked. "What if . . . what if we're on our own, I mean, decision-wise, but we have laws to guide us. And maybe those are divinely inspired, like Isaac says."

"So you want to start to keep kosher now?" Josh chided me. "Better not pierce anything," he said under his breath.

And then suddenly all the voices around me faded. They continued to argue. But as I sat there I realized that my Judaism *could* mean something. Something practical. Something useful. A way to think about things. To make choices. I mean, two days ago I hadn't thought about piercing or even a boyfriend as a real choice. But it was. *Maybe*, just maybe, I didn't belong with my old friends, because I didn't really *like* what they were doing, I wasn't interested in the same things, I didn't want to feel pressured to be exactly like them. I took a gulp of air. Wow. I thought about Isaac. Maybe I did want a boyfriend, but not the one my friends had chosen for me. Not one they'd even approve of.

I think that dream changed me. I'm trying to be honest here—I *know* it did. If I can wrestle with an angel or if I have an angel inside me, then everything about me is precious, isn't it? There's a truth inside me, inside all of us. I caught a glimpse of it. And that truth is mystery. And maybe, for me, *that's* the essence of God. Mystery. And maybe this is the beginning of a very long wrestling match.

Interview ～ CAROL MATAS

Your first four books were science fiction. When did your Jewish background begin to play a role in your writing?

It wasn't until my family was living in Montreal and my husband was working at the Jewish Community Centre that a friend gave me a book that began the change in my writing. My husband, who had been born in Denmark, had begun telling me stories about his family, especially his father, who had been only twelve years old when Germany invaded Denmark. By the time my father-in-law was fifteen, he was a full-fledged member of the Danish resistance. I'd decided to write a novel about that when I was given a book about the rescue of the Danish Jews in Denmark. I'd been taught about the Holocaust, naturally (one of the main reasons I didn't believe in God), and yet I'd never been told the story of the amazing Danish people who'd saved almost the entire Jewish population of Denmark. I knew I had to write about it. That book, *Lisa's War*, led to my being asked to write *Daniel's Story* for the United States Holocaust Memorial Museum. And that book changed my life. It changed my writing, my beliefs, and I found myself on a new path, my Jewishness becoming central to my writing. I wanted to write about the Jewish experience, not just about the Holocaust, but also in contemporary books, like *The Freak*, and in historicals, like *The Garden*.

You say that book changed your beliefs. In what way?

We never know what life is going to bring us or what will be important to us in the future. When I was a teenager I had no idea that either my Jewishness or writing would be so important to me now. In fact, I never dreamed I'd be a writer—and my Judaism was something I took for granted. I grew up in a city where I never encountered anti-Semitism, with a father who never stopped bragging about the achievements of Jewish people—in the arts, politics, science, etc. I was happy to be Jewish. I had a Bat Mitzvah and instead of gifts I asked for trees to be planted in Israel. I was active in the B'nai B'rith Youth Organization, one year as president of my chapter. I also took ballet three times a week, hung out with my friends, mooned over boys, talked on the phone for hours, and read voraciously. Being Jewish was simply one part of my life. I'm still not religious in the traditional way, but I have a deep belief in "the One" and I believe that every single person is a soul with the capacity to choose good, and to refuse to live in fear and hatred.

The issue of choice is central to your story "Wrestling with Angels." Is that where the story began for you?
Dreams have played an important part in my path as a writer, so it was, perhaps, natural that Jaci is also pushed by her dreams to examine her life. All my writing deals with the issue of choice in some way—our lives are full of choices, we must think for ourselves, decide for ourselves, never just follow (as the Germans did in Nazi Germany), and try to mend or repair the world we live in.

Biography ∽ CAROL MATAS

Carol Matas is the author of more than two dozen books. She writes science fiction, fantasy (especially with her co-author, Perry Nodelman), contemporary fiction, and historical fiction. She is particularly well known for her series of World War II and Holocaust books, beginning with *Lisa's War* and *Code Name Kris*. She wrote *Daniel's Story* for the United States Holocaust Memorial Museum in Washington, D.C., and since then has written *After the War*, and the sequel, *The Garden*, about children who survived the Holocaust; *Greater than Angels*, about Jewish children helped by the people of a small French village; and *In My Enemy's House*, about a Polish Jewish girl who survives the war by living with a Nazi family. Among Ms. Matas's many honors are Sydney Taylor Awards for *Lisa's War* and *Sworn Enemies*, and Jewish Book Awards (Toronto) for *After the War* and *The Garden*. Many of her books have also been ALA Quick Picks, New York Public Library Books for the Teen Age, and Reader's Choice Award winners.

The Heart of Buchanan

by Sandy Asher

The way to Buchanan's heart, I thought, was through its middle school chorus.

Five minutes into the first day of school, while I was fussing with the combination to my new locker, a girl's voice behind me shrieked out the clue: "You're going to *Chicago*? The *entire* middle school chorus?"

"We won our spot in the competition," a calmer voice replied. "Now we just have to raise enough money to get there."

I turned and caught sight of matching blond ponytails bobbing down the hall side by side. No time for shyness. I forced myself into step behind them.

"Luck-yyyyyy!" the shorter, louder girl squealed. "I wish I could sing. Chorus is so cool. Pom-pom squad never does anything fun like going to Chicago. We just follow the team around and freeze our butts off while they lose one game after another."

"Excuse me," I said, tapping the taller girl on the shoulder. "About the middle school chorus? I just moved to Buchanan, and I love to sing. Am I too late to audition?"

The two blondes eyed me up and down, as I knew they would. My dad's in the army and we relocate every two or three years. I've been the "new girl" so often, I have the routine down to a science. "What kind of life is that for a Jewish family," my grandma says, each time we move, "schlepping from one place to another?" But Dad reminds her that wandering certainly is a Jewish tradition, and the free medical school education silences all debate. "My son, the army doctor" is close enough to "my son, the doctor" for full bragging rights in Brooklyn.

Anyway, Buchanan was our first Midwest assignment, with the smallest base we'd been to so far, and the smallest town we'd ever lived in. Nearly every kid scooting around the three of us in the hall had straight blond hair. And then there was me, with my dark brown curls and an olive complexion half a world away from their golden, late-summer tans.

We were warned before we arrived: We'd be the only Jewish family in town.

"Find your way in," Dad commanded.

I got right to work. Thinking twice about it only makes it harder. I figure there are two ways to approach cold water: inch your way in and shiver a long time, or take a running dive and get it over with. I'd learned how to dive.

The two girls might have gone on giving me the once-over forever, but I broke into their trance with another try: "My name's Sarah Goldstein. My dad's stationed at Fort Gray. We just moved here from D.C."

Blank stares.

"Washington? The capital?"

The taller girl finally snapped out of it. "Oh, hi," she said. "I'm Traci Morgan and this is DeeDee Campbell. Are you in eighth grade?"

I nodded.

"Mrs. Taylor's homeroom?"

I nodded again.

"Cool!" Traci said. "Then you're with us. Come on, we'll show you the way. So, you moved here from Washington?"

"Have you ever met Chelsea Clinton?" DeeDee asked, suspiciously, as if that would prove my claim.

"No," I said, "but I once saw her cat on the White House lawn."

I'd found my way in. Traci would lead me to chorus and other friends, and I'd be home free. We Goldsteins are trained to it. "We're going to be on the move a lot," I remember Mom explaining, the first time I had to leave one school and start all over again in another. "Look around. Find your way in. You'll never want for friends or interesting things to do."

No problem for her, or for Dad. Given half a chance, they could make friends with a tree stump. No problem for me, either, once I got the hang of it. But then there's Molly, my little sister. She's in third grade. It was bound to happen, I guess, that a Goldstein would come along who didn't take to life on the road as easily as the rest of us, and Molly was it. She loved her school in D.C. and couldn't understand why she had to leave it and all her friends behind. It just about broke her heart.

I could tell she was scared stiff when I dropped her off at her classroom that first morning, even though she was keeping up a brave front, "soldiering on," as Dad would say. Luckily, Buchanan Elementary and Buchanan Middle School are really just two wings of the same building.

"Look, Molly, I'll be right over there," I pointed out. "Maybe we'll even pass each other in the halls or the cafeteria. Promise you'll wave?"

"Okay," she said, her brown eyes measuring the width of the building, the maximum distance between us. And then, again, more confidently, "Okay."

Actually, it would do me some good to see her in the halls, too, more than I cared to admit. When you move around a lot, your family is the only thing that holds steady. It took some help from her teacher, Mrs. Rose, to peel Molly off me at the third grade classroom door, but maybe I wasn't letting go of her damp little hand all that willingly, either.

"Find your way in." While Molly did the best she could, I focused on my target: In no time at all, I'd sung for Mr. Blake, the music teacher, won myself a place in the alto section of the chorus, and, much to DeeDee Campbell's annoyance, suddenly had more in common with Traci than she did. I never meant to come between them, but that's the way it goes sometimes. People grow apart. I thought my best friend in San Francisco and I would write, call, and E-mail each other for the rest of our lives, but we didn't. After a couple of months, we just stopped. No hard feelings. Of course, I didn't have to watch while she grew close to a new best friend, and DeeDee did.

Traci and I tried to include her, but we had the "raising money for Chicago" thing to worry about, rehearsals to attend, music to learn. We didn't mean to burst into song together while DeeDee stood there looking hurt. It just happened now and then. Traci and I hung out with the same people three afternoons a week. If Mr. Blake belched during warm-ups on Monday, could we help it if we were still chuckling over it the next morning? So it wasn't that funny if you weren't there to hear it—does that mean three people can't *all* be best friends? Traci and I were willing. DeeDee was not.

By the end of September, she'd found a way to get back at me. The High Holy Days arrived. I'd have to miss school for Rosh Hashanah and Yom Kippur. Dad, Mom, Molly, and I would drive to Springfield, eighty miles away, to attend the nearest temple.

DeeDee reacted to the news with her trademark shriek: "I didn't know you were *Jewish!* I've never met anyone who was *Jewish.*"

The entire lunchroom population, cooks included, turned around to stare at us.

"Does that mean you're not a Christian?" a boy at the table next to ours piped up.

"That's right."

"You don't believe in Jesus Christ?"

"I believe he existed. I don't believe he's God."

"Then you can't go to Heaven."

I took a deep breath and sucked in the urge to tell him I'd rather not if bigots like him were going to be there. As I whirled back toward my own table, I couldn't help noticing DeeDee's smirk at the thought of me weeping outside the pearly gates. Or better yet, frying to a crisp.

Traci, on the other hand, regarded me with fear and pity in her wide blue eyes. "You mean you haven't ever been saved?"

I tried to explain: "Getting into Heaven is not a big concern of ours. We concentrate on being good and doing good here on earth."

Her look softened to a thoughtful frown. "That . . . that sounds . . . okay."

DeeDee pursed her lips in disgust, and all around us debates burst out like brush fires: Was I doomed? Or, if I wasn't a Christian to begin with, did the rules even apply to me?

I stayed out of it, hoping the novelty would wear off soon. I figured if Traci stuck with me, I'd be all right. Let it go, I told myself, let it go.

And it went. After the High Holy Days, interest in my Jewishness faded. I could sense there were kids who steered clear of my company, and Traci informed me that some ministers around town were really adamant about the evils of not "accepting Jesus Christ as your personal savior." But all in all, I became a curiosity when anyone thought about it, and most of the time, no one did.

Then winter blew into town. Full force.

Snowflakes replaced turkeys on bulletin boards around school. Tinsel framed the window of the principal's office and the doorway to Mrs. Taylor's homeroom. A miniature Christmas tree appeared in a corner behind her desk, complete with tiny decorations.

"That's nothing," Dad said, when I told him about it after school. "There's a crèche on the courthouse lawn."

"Isn't that illegal?" Mom asked.

"What's a crèche?" Molly wanted to know.

"Statues," I told her. "Of Mary and Joseph and baby Jesus."

"We have a crèche," Molly said, happily. "Under the tree in our classroom."

Mom and Dad exchanged perturbed looks. "Hoooo-boy," Dad said. "Welcome to the Bible Belt."

"Is it something bad?" Molly asked. "Are crèches bad?"

"No, sweetheart," Dad said. "They're not bad, but they really belong in churches, or people's homes, not public schools. Crèches are for Christians, and not everyone in a classroom is Christian."

Mom gathered Molly onto her lap. "Like us, sweetie," she said.

"We're Jewish. We don't have a crèche because we don't celebrate Christmas."

"We celebrated Christmas in D.C.," I reminded them all. "And in San Francisco before that. We sang carols in school. It was fun."

"You sang Hanukkah songs, too," Mom pointed out. "And songs about Kwanzaa. Is your chorus here learning any of those?"

"No," I had to admit.

"Try suggesting it," Dad advised me.

Easier said than done.

"But the eighth grade chorus does the exact same program every year," Traci told me, when I ran the idea past her. "My mom and dad did it when *they* were in eighth grade. With the same robes and the same candles and the same carols in the same order. It's a tradition. Everyone looks forward to it."

She wasn't mad. Just shocked that I'd want to change a program everybody else in town loved.

I reported her reaction to Mom and Dad. "Do I still have to talk to Mr. Blake about it?" I asked.

Dad shook his head. "Buchanan was Buchanan long before we arrived."

"Meaning what?" Mom asked.

"Meaning we're not going to change it."

"And Sarah and Molly?" Mom asked. "Is it going to change them?"

"They know who they are," Dad assured her. "Singing carols won't make them Christian any more than singing opera would make them Italian."

So, it was settled. Molly and I knew who we were.

Problem was, nobody else did.

"Got your tree up yet?" Traci asked one morning on the way to homeroom.

"We don't have a tree," I told her.

"Why not?"

"We don't celebrate Christmas."

That worried frown creased her forehead again. "Not at all?"

"Not even a little."

"So what *do* you do?"

The warning bell rang, cutting short the time I'd need to explain that we didn't feel we had to do anything. We do celebrate Hanukkah around the same time of year, but it's a minor festival, not the "Jewish Christmas." Rather than get into all that, I just said, "Nothing."

"No Christmas shopping?" she pressed on, as we slid into our seats. "No presents? No lights? No Santa?"

I shook my head.

"I can't imagine that!"

The intercom crackled and sputtered to life as our principal cranked up his morning announcement routine. Only this time, he started off with the jingle of sleigh bells and a jolly "Ho-ho-ho, Buchanan students! Merrrrrrry Christmas!"

Traci grinned. "Well, at least you get to celebrate Christmas at school," she said. "That's lucky!"

It went on. If I had a dollar for every "Christmas tree up yet?" or "Ready for Christmas yet?" or "Done your Christmas shopping yet?" I heard over the next couple of weeks, I could buy a whole bunch of people some really major gifts.

But the worst of it came one afternoon when I arrived at Molly's classroom door to walk her to the bus before chorus practice. Her face was streaked with tears.

I knelt and swooped her into my arms, parka, book bag, and all. "What's wrong? What happened? Molly? Tell me!"

For a minute or two, she kept her face buried in my neck and sobbed. Then she finally squirmed to be let go and pulled herself together enough to talk.

"Our student teacher made up a Christmas play for the assembly. She told us to kneel by the crèche and welcome baby Jesus. I said I didn't want to do that, and she said, 'Why not?' and I said because I was Jewish and crèches are for Christians. And then she got all upset. She said, 'It's just a play.' And Mrs. Rose and all the other kids said the same thing. They wouldn't listen! So I didn't know what to do." As she thought about what happened next, her face crinkled up again and her voice got all squeaky. "So I knelt by the crèche and welcomed baby Jesus. But I didn't want to!"

I calmed her down as best I could and got her on the bus with a promise to talk later, then raced over to chorus practice. Just as we launched into "O Come, All Ye Faithful," a sickly, sweaty feeling crept over me, kind of half guilt and half anger. But what was I guilty of? Who was I angry at? I looked around the room. I saw how I fit right in, how no one would notice a bit of difference between me and the other singers. That was a good thing, wasn't it? *I'd found my way in.* So why was this suddenly bothering me?

Then I pictured Molly kneeling in front of that crèche, and I knew what my sickly feeling was all about.

When I got home after practice, Mom and Dad were seated at the kitchen table, with Molly snuggled up in Mom's lap. They all wore long faces, so I knew Molly had repeated her story. I slid into the empty chair opposite Dad.

"So? What are we going to do?" Mom was asking him.

Dad shook his head. "We've got eighteen months to go in this town."

"She's not going to kneel down and welcome baby Jesus," Mom insisted, "and that's final."

"I don't want to be the only one," Molly whimpered. "I don't want to be the only one left out."

"But you don't want to do the play, either, do you, Molly?" I asked.

"No," she said, and hiccuped from all her sobbing.

"How can they put a child in this position?" Mom asked, stroking the damp curls away from Molly's face. "They're *educators.* What can they possibly be *thinking?*"

"They just don't get it," I said. "They can't imagine not having Christmas, or not wanting to if you don't. That's exactly what Traci said, 'I can't imagine that.' And *she* was really *trying.*"

"That's one advantage of being in the minority," Dad observed.

"You never make the mistake of believing everybody thinks the same way you do!"

"I'm not in charge of what they can or can't imagine," Mom insisted. "I'm in charge of my daughter. And I'm calling Mrs. Rose in the morning."

"What are you going to say?" Molly asked.

Mom caught the fear in Molly's voice and slammed the brakes on her own anger. "Well . . . how about . . . that maybe you and I could help change the play?"

"We *can't* change the play!" Molly wailed.

"Why not?" Dad asked.

"Because we just *can't*! Because *that's the way they want it*!"

Mom's mouth opened for a second and snapped shut again.

"It's just like the chorus program," I pointed out.

Mom unclenched her jaw long enough to say, "I will speak with Mrs. Rose."

Then the subject was dropped till morning.

True to her word, Mom was on the phone to Mrs. Rose before our bus came. And she was more frustrated than ever when she reported their conversation: "The woman got all *huffy*," she said, imitating a Mrs. Rose turned shrill and thorny. "She had *no idea* that Christmas put pressure on our child. Molly need not be in the play, she assured me, she can spend rehearsal time in another room. She can sit out of music classes, too, if we find Christmas carols *offensive*." Mom threw her hands heavenward in frustration. "I shouldn't have called. I've gone too far. I may have done more harm than good!"

She shot Dad an anguished look over Molly's head, but I knew exactly what she was thinking: Molly had finally settled into her new school. She hadn't said a word about Washington since Thanksgiving. And now this.

"It's the play that's gone too far," Dad pointed out. "But, I don't know, maybe this just isn't a battle an eight-year-old should have to fight."

"Not *all alone*," Mom agreed.

And that's when Molly and I had to leave them and trudge off to the bus stop.

"Are you going to do the assembly?" I asked her.

"I don't know," she said. "I don't want to, but I don't want to be the only one left out."

Chorus practice was in high gear after school. Besides the assembly program coming up on the last day before winter break (or "Christmas vacation," as everyone in Buchanan called it), we were scheduled to perform for the Downtown Business Association's monthly breakfast meeting, with the idea in mind that the splendor of our presentation would inspire them to kick in a nice donation toward our trip to Chicago.

So the pressure was on, and Mr. Blake was out to beat his own world record for nitpicking. Along with our singing, everything from hair to posture to a wayward stick of gum was subject to lectures on pride and professionalism. The mood was tense, but we sang our hearts out—and we sounded *great*. I'd never felt so much a part of a group in all my years of school hopping.

I'd never felt so rotten, either.

One thing about inching your way into cold water—if you don't like it, you have time to change your mind and turn around. A dive takes you under, for better or worse. Sure, that student teacher's play had gone too far. And maybe Mom shouldn't have made that phone call. But what about me? Had I really found my way into Buchanan Middle School? Or had I lost my way altogether? I was a voice in a carefully blended chorus of voices, but not one single person I'd met since I arrived in town had the slightest idea of who that voice belonged to. And who was I, really? Someone who knew how to fit in? Was that all that could be said for me?

Even little Molly had tried to make her student teacher listen, and I was old enough to make choices she couldn't even understand. I'd had my Bat Mitzvah in D.C.; I'd announced to family and friends that I was ready to act like a responsible Jewish adult. Instead, I'd dived in headfirst, and then it was too late. So I smiled and stayed quiet, letting

Buchanan believe whatever it wanted about me: that I'd get my Christmas tree put up eventually; that I'd finish my Christmas shopping soon; or that I secretly wished I could.

Eighteen months to go. The chorus and Chicago—or not. Traci—or maybe no friends at all. Molly and me together—or all alone. Before I even realized I'd made my choice, I stopped singing. Right between "night" and "holy."

Mr. Blake noticed immediately and tapped his baton on the music stand. A hush fell over the room. "Sarah? Is there a problem?"

I stepped down off the risers and moved toward him. It seemed to take forever. Stern impatience tugged down the corners of his mouth as I slowly closed the distance between us.

"I can't do this," I told him in a whispery voice I barely recognized as my own.

"Do what?" he asked. "You can't do what?"

"I can't be in the Christmas program."

He tilted his head forward so that his gray green eyes peered at me over his reading glasses. For obvious reasons, he was struck dumb.

"I'm Jewish," I went on. "This is not what I believe. The only way I can hope to make anyone understand that is to stop singing."

Mr. Blake measured his response out very slowly. "Do you realize, young lady, that we are scheduled to perform for the Downtown Business Association tomorrow morning, and that our trip to Chicago depends on it? Do you realize you are disrupting our plans and undermining our hard work with this . . . this . . . *protest?*"

"I know," I said. "I'm sorry."

"I will not allow you back into chorus after Christmas," he informed me.

I nodded, swallowing hard to hold back the tears. Before I left the room, I glanced up toward Traci. Was there anything more than surprise on her face, same as all the others? Hard to tell.

Maybe over the next eighteen months, some of them would begin to understand. Or maybe not. But Mom and Dad were both right: This was not a battle eight-year-olds should have to fight. Not *all alone.*

I didn't really start shaking until I got out in the hall. But it was okay; I'd done what I had to do. *So much for the heart of Buchanan, I* thought. *I've found the way back to my own.*

Interview ✐ SANDY ASHER

Where did you get the idea for this story?
During the High Holy Days, soldiers from a nearby fort attend services at our temple. At first, there were only two or three of them, but last year they filled a row. They set me to thinking about the contrast between growing up Jewish in a large city like Philadelphia, as I did, with many huge congregations to choose from, and here in Springfield, where we have one statistically tiny, but close-knit, community of Jewish families. Individual responsibility takes on a whole new importance when there really is no one else to take up the slack if you turn away.

How else has growing up Jewish been reflected in your writing?
My experience was schizoid in several ways. My old neighborhood in Philadelphia was a "melting pot" of immigrants and minorities, Jewish and non-Jewish, but what was important to everybody back then—the forties and fifties—was to be American. So we celebrated "American holidays" along with our own traditions and nobody thought twice about it. My grandparents, observant Jews who immigrated from Russia, bought me chocolate bunnies and toy chicks around Easter time, and at school, everyone sang carols in December, although many of the teachers leading the singing were Jewish as well.

I have precious memories of family Seders, lighting Hanukkah candles, and sitting next to my father in *shul* for hours as a little girl, pretending to chant Hebrew prayers I didn't understand. But I also experienced an entirely different Judaism—heavy with guilt, obligation, and superstition. I remember wondering, "Does God really get that angry at a child who eats a candy bar during Pesach? Or takes the wrong knife out of the wrong drawer to spread cream cheese?" If so, I wanted none of it.

After a period of rebellion, I found—and continue to find, as in editing this anthology—my own ways to connect to the rich cultural, ethical, historical, and religious heritage of our people, and I think that effort is reflected in my writing. I've published poems, short stories, two young adult novels, and two plays that grew specifically out of my Jewish background, the tragedy of it, the comedy of it, and everything in between. I learned about the effects of the Holocaust on children of survivors while writing my second novel, *Daughters of the Law*, and made a study of Jewish humor—of which there is plenty!—for the research that went into my play *The Wise Men of Chelm*. But all of my work, whether the characters, plots, and themes are recognizably Jewish or not, is a direct outgrowth of a very Jewish, ongoing, and often heated discussion with God and humanity about how best to live in this world.

Biography ⟿ SANDY ASHER

Sandy Asher grew up in Philadelphia, but has spent her adult life in the Midwest, earning a B.A. from Indiana University and moving to Springfield, Missouri, in 1967. As writer-in-residence at Drury College, she directs workshops and contests for writers of all ages. Among her seven young adult novels, *Summer Begins* and *Daughters of the Law* are of special Jewish interest. Other books include *Where Do You Get Your Ideas?*, for young writers, and the fiction anthology *But That's Another Story*, which she edited. The recipient of an NEA grant in playwriting, Ms. Asher has been honored with the American Alliance for Theater and Education's Distinguished Play Award, an "Outstanding Play for Young Audiences" citation by the International Association of Theaters for Children and Young People, the IUPUI/Bonderman Award, a Kennedy Center New Visions/New Voices selection, and the Joseph Campbell Memorial Award. *The Wise Men of Chelm*, based on Jewish folktales, was recently chosen for the anthology *Theater for Young Audiences: 20 Great Plays for Children*. Ms. Asher and her husband, Harvey, a history professor, are the parents of two grown children, Emily and Ben.

About MAZON:
A Jewish Response to Hunger

MAZON ("food" in Hebrew) provides cash grants to a broad spectrum of nonprofit organizations working to confront the tragedy of hunger, primarily in the United States, but also in Israel and in impoverished countries. Its dual purpose is to provide for those who are hungry today, as well as to help alleviate the poverty that causes hunger. MAZON has provided grants—more than $16 million to hundreds of programs since its founding in 1985—to the very best anti-hunger agencies worldwide without discrimination against race, religion, or other false barriers. MAZON's grants help agencies provide both short-term, immediate intervention and long-term solutions aimed at lifting people permanently out of their impoverished circumstances.

MAZON asks American Jews to continue the ancient Jewish tradition of feeding the hungry by:

- sharing the joy of festive occasions by contributing 3% of the cost of life-cycle celebrations, such as bar and bat mitzvahs, weddings, and other special days. MAZON table cards are an easy, unobtrusive way to tell your guests that you are sharing celebrations with those in need;

- contributing at Yom Kippur—the most solemn day of the Jewish year—the money that would have been spent on food during the single day of voluntary fasting, to help feed those whose fast shows no sign of ending;

- at Passover, letting "one who is hungry enter and eat" by giving to MAZON the amount of money that would have been spent to invite one extra person to the Seder table;

- giving to MAZON to commemorate happy occasions in the lives of friends and family members, or to honor the memory of loved ones.

To contribute to MAZON or for further information, contact:

MAZON: A Jewish Response to Hunger
12401 Wilshire Boulevard, Suite 303
Los Angeles, CA 90025-1015

Phone: (310) 442-0020

Fax: (310) 442-0030

e-mail: mazonmail@aol.com

www.shamash.org